HIDDEN VIRTUE

HIDDEN VIRTUE

Hidden Justice Book Four

NOLON KING

DAIVD W. WRIGHT

STERLING & STONE

To YOU, the reader.
Thank you for your support.
Thank you for the wonderful emails.
Thank you for the thoughtful reviews.
Thank you for reading and loving our stories.

Chapter One

THE SMALL MOUND next to the fence was covered in creeping weeds. Drooping wildflowers. The sun pulling all the color out of everything like a curling, desaturated photo.

Frank rarely came back here. He didn't think it was fair to Sarah for him to stand at Carmen's grave. Especially since he had stopped visiting the others.

Just the occasional token effort to keep it clean. Scrape the bird droppings off the crooked concrete cross. Clean a path along the fence. Rake up the dead oak leaves scattered all around.

Besides, he could see her from his room in the barn. A hot loft over a broad open area full of vehicles under tarps and yard tools. A tiny deck hanging from the side was just big enough for his camp chair and cooler.

He often visited some of the places from his history. Driving by Heirloom Cove to see how they had replaced his house with a modern ranch that didn't fit in with the neighborhood aesthetic. Wood and stone instead of tile and stucco.

Out at the Willet County Business Park where he would skirt the front gate to drive through the parking lot. A big loop ending at the fence behind where Stan's gym used to be.

The nature reserve had eaten every sign that had ever even been past the chain link. A wild encroachment of vegetation that would soon overtake the top of the fence and start spilling down into the parking lot.

He even took a weekend every now and then to cruise over to Playa Dolor. Sit on the beach and drink the tide in.

Frank Grimm had no fear of being recognized. He looked nothing like the two men he used to be. The retired family man looking for his daughter was long gone. Consigned to a past of pain and broken promises.

The delusional beach Frank was gone too. Gained muscle and strength washed away in alcohol. Neat white beard trimmed into a scraggly goatee. Bald head grown back into an unkempt mop.

But a boot to the face had changed him far more than any disguise. Broken nose healed into a grotesque crook of bone and flesh. Split eyebrow healed into a scar that made his upper eyelid droop at an angle that obscured his vision on his right side.

His clothes — typically a pair of khaki cargo shorts, an open tropical shirt, and jute flip-flops — hung from his leaned body to flap like an empty sail.

Days spent in the barn. Working on the Dodge van. On the computer doing research. Drinking too much.

Mo and Gen had stopped trying to engage with him. Left Frank to his own devices. He was getting to the bottom of the bag of cash Carmen had made him take from her alligator smuggling van — or endangered turtles. He had never really looked that deeply into it.

He wasn't worried about the money. He only needed enough to finish.

How many months had it been since he last saw Stan? He hadn't counted. Stopped waiting a long time ago. Mo said his cousin was okay. Why would he lie?

Frank looked back over his shoulder at where Mo stood next to the orange RV. Soaping it up for its weekly washing. Gen jumped out from the shadow at the rear bumper to spray Mo with the hose, and Frank could hear her giggle all the way from his watching place.

His gaze drifted to the wheelchair at the edge of the gravel. GG sat in the sun. A diminished version of the human wrecking ball he used to be. The doctors said his end was fast approaching, but Frank wanted to focus on other things.

There was pain all over. Too much for him to heed it all. Frank had to pick and choose, so he focused back on Carmen's grave.

He wondered if anybody missed her. If she was even *worth* being missed. He tried to miss her, but instead, he kept missing the man he had been when with her. Missed the way she made him feel.

He shook his head in bitter resentment. Aimed squarely at himself. Then tipped his beer up to drain the rest of the bottle. Warm and foamy, but there was plenty more back in the barn.

He dropped the empty into the tallest clump of weeds. A flutter of bugs flew up at the disturbance. Like when Mo cut the grass. Stirred up the insects that brought the birds.

One black cloud leading to another.

He shook his head with a sigh. Dropped down to fish the bottle out. Stayed on his knees to pull at the weeds and vines covering the mound.

The sun tracked by. Exposing his back to the unseasonal heat. The skin on his neck. The scalp not covered by his thinning hair. Hands and forearms. All darkening into old leather.

He took his shirt off to avoid worsening his farmer's tan. Hung it on a barb in the fence. Went back to his impromptu landscaping.

He used his hands as the tools. Cleared the weeds. Pulled the grass. Scooped and shaped the loose dirt. In a widening circle to join the manicured lawn outside the border of her grave.

Until it matched the rest of the yard.

Then he straightened the cross. Pressed it deeper into the ground.

Collected the armloads of waste. Scattered it all on the compost pile behind the barn. Wiped the worst of the dirt from his hands and knees. Grabbed a frosty Corona and went back to retrieve his shirt.

Like guilt chipping away at resolve, he knew the weeds would be back. And eventually, he'd break down and clear it up again. He wasn't even sure if she deserved this much care. He only knew her as she was with him.

Lying to him the way he had lied to her.

But the same way nature covered up crimes, she also uncovered flaws. Exposed painful truths. She would come back to reclaim the grave as she always did, and he wondered what else she would uncover in the process.

Some new insight into how poorly he had lived his life.

He smiled at his own dramatic melancholy. Hung the shirt over his shoulder before going back to his room in the barn.

A couple peanut butter and jelly sandwiches before he opened his evening's bottle of bourbon. Scribble a few final notes in his journal. Got to bed a bit earlier than usual.

Tomorrow started the beginning of the end. He wanted to be ready.

Chapter Two

FRANK COULD TELL Mo was shocked when he agreed to the group therapy session. The way he paused before smiling. The way his eyes narrowed.

Once a week, Mo had a group of veterans come to the property, and they'd set up in a circle with a shrink. Frank had never bothered to remember his name.

Every time, Mo asked, and every time, Frank declined. He'd listened plenty of times. They always made camp in the barn. On the concrete half where the cars were. Water and iced tea, and clouds of cigarette smoke drifting up to his little balcony.

Men and women who could use some help for sure. Like Stan. Like *Frank* — a little. Many who were victims of circumstance. Put in a war they didn't believe in or weren't prepared for. PTSD. Unable to drive down the street without swerving away from every garbage bag fluttering on the curb.

They came, and the doctor started the session with some gentle words of welcome, and then he'd open up the floor to someone who wanted to share their story. Frank noticed it was often the same three or four — patients? participants? — talking, while most of the others just listened.

The two hours would end, then the doctor would conclude with a drawn-out statement that smacked of the corporate optimism of a poster caption, then they'd mill around, talking shop. Reminiscing in reverent tones about the very thing that was now ruining their lives.

Frank knew he was also a victim. Owens had admitted as much when he had put him in the back of the van for questioning. Targeting Frank's daughter for no other reason than her being a beautiful little girl. And if bad things happened to good people, then what Frank went through was *nothing* compared to what Jenny had been forced to endure.

And that's where Frank diverged from the group. They were struggling to overcome the weight keeping them below the waves; *he* was trying to breathe underwater.

He had come to the conclusion that he deserved the suffering. That his current position was *his* fault. A cynical, defeatist attitude, but one that served his goals.

To die while killing Detective Owens and anybody that got in his way.

That thought always made him smile, but the dour faces around him reminded him of how inappropriate that might be.

A young man with scars on his neck and face — skin grafts to repair damage from mortar fire fragments — leaned forward in his metal folding chair. Wiped the tears poised on his lower eyelids. "I see it happening, you know?"

Frank looked up at the rough beams of the ceiling. Tried to remember the young man's name.

"There's this part of me that lashes out, you know? Then there's this other part of me that sees me doing it."

Miguel. That was his name. Frank nodded to himself. Took a noisy sip of his iced tea.

Heavily laced with tequila.

"So now I'm getting even *more* pissed," Miguel continued. "Because I'm trying to stop from yelling more, you know? Like I'm there in my head screaming at myself to just fucking quit it, but I can't, and that pisses me off *more*, and there's nobody else there but Marie, so I lash out at whatever, you know? At *her*."

Miguel leaned back for a deep breath. Sagged as he sighed it back out. "I ain't hit her yet, but I feel like it's coming. Just like last time. And what happens if the nightmares start up again? Will I go loco on her if she tries to wake me up cuz I'm shouting in my sleep?"

An uncomfortable shuffling from all around.

The doctor — barrel-chested, bearded, and tattooed — held his hands up, like he was waiting for a double high five. "We've said it before." His voice was soft and smooth. The shocking opposite of his appearance. "Nothing is *inevitable*. Possible, yes. Perhaps even *probable*, but that doesn't mean it's a forgone conclusion."

Miguel wiped his nose on the back of his fist. "I know, but I can see it happening, and I can't *stop*."

The shrink kept his hands in front of him. "But the last time, you said you weren't even aware of what you were doing. That Marie would try to tell you that you were being irrational, and *that* would make you lash out. You're saying that you are now able to recognize the behavior when it happens instead of *after* the fact. You don't think that's progress? You don't think you are veering away from the unavoidable?"

Frank figured that *everything* was unavoidable, but he felt that sentiment wouldn't go over well with this audience. He covered his smile with a drink. Glanced up to see Mo watching him and barely suppressed his defensive shrug.

Frank had felt plenty guilty for a few weeks. He saw Mo and Gen out here in the middle of nowhere as some kind of exile, but in reality, they were living an accelerated goal. One that their insistence on helping him had forced them to pursue.

It was easy for him to transfer his guilt to their blame.

Except for the weekly visitors — men and women that Frank refused to make more than strangers — GG was the only other person there. And that sweet, gentle man was dying.

One of the few things that made Frank feel ... *anything* more than just sorry for himself.

Mo worked on the orange RV a little each week, and it was near completion. Restored and renewed, it was down to some exterior repairs, and then? Frank suspected they were just waiting for GG to finally pass. The last thing holding them to this property.

He had heard them talking about how they could do this anywhere. *This* was presumably the group therapy. Going to where the problems were instead of making the problems come to them.

On the road, but off the grid. Maybe start a family someday.

All things that Frank could get behind, but there was something about GG — a projection of his own guilt — that made him resentful of their dreams. He knew it was irrational. Like Miguel, he recognized it as it happened, and still sneered at their decision with derision and scorn.

They didn't say it, but to them, GG's death meant freedom.

After the session wrapped up, Frank stood for a quiet

escape. Maybe up to his loft for a fresh drink. Before he could make it out of the circle, the psychologist intercepted him with an extended hand and an open smile. "Glad to see Mo finally got you down here. I've seen you watching. I'm Rogers."

Frank took the offered hand. Squeezed and pumped. "I'm Grimm."

The smile became a grin, and Rogers nodded. "I can tell."

Frank reclaimed his hand. One of the other patients came by surrounded by a cloud of greasy vapor. The artificial banana bread aroma made his eyes water. He would have preferred more cigarette smoke. "It's just my name," he said, wondering why he had used the real one.

Rogers kept the power of his grin fixed on Frank. "I understand. It was just a joke."

Frank nodded. "So how long you been running this show?"

Rogers brushed the question away with a flap of his hand. "My story isn't that interesting. I'd like to hear *yours*, though."

Frank smiled. "I'm sure you've heard it already. Or one like it. I'll not bore you with my problems."

Rogers' grin faded into polite interest. "So, you *do* have problems?"

"Don't we all?"

Rogers nodded. "It has been my experience, yes."

"So, you have problems too, then."

Rogers closed his eyes as if conceding a point. Frank took the moment as a distraction to turn away, only to run into a solid wall of dark flesh.

"My man," Mo said, but the excitement that used to accompany his usual greeting was gone. "You may not see it, but this is a step. Maybe not a big one, but it's in the right direction."

Frank smiled. "It's that kind of encouragement that continues to solidify our friendship." He tipped up the last of his iced tea, but couldn't keep eye contact. Frank's heart wasn't in the jest, and by the look on Mo's face, neither was his.

"Come on. What's it gonna take?"

Frank took a step back to keep from feeling Mo looming over him. "What's *what* gonna take?"

His gaze flickered over Frank's shoulder. Like he was getting permission from the shrink to continue. Then he brought it back and focused on Frank's forehead instead of his eyes. Drew a deep breath, like he was about to say something with effort.

Frank didn't let him start. "You talking about happiness, Mo? Or ... engagement? Or my own self-destructive behavior?"

Mo's shoulders sagged like a giant wilting flower.

Rogers' voice made Frank whirl around. "Let's start with the last one."

Frank rolled his eyes. "Let's not."

"Why not? We're here to help."

Frank shook his head with a sigh. "I'm not here to be helped. I don't *want* to be helped. But some people think *they* want to help."

"Don't we?"

The man's even demeanor was infuriating. Frank snorted laughter. "*We*? I know you just as much as you know me."

"I've wanted to change that for some time."

"But that's just *it*," Frank shouted. "I don't *want* to know you."

The sudden quiet all around them was like pressure

against the sides of his head. Frank nodded with finality. "I'll tell you the same thing I told him." He cocked his thumb over his shoulder at Mo. "I want to kill the man that raped and murdered my daughter. The man that hurt her so bad, it took *days* to catalogue every cut and bruise. The man that drove me from my wife. Made her kill herself. The man that ruined my life."

Rogers' eyes were like wet glass. Like tears about to fall. "And who is that man, Grimm?"

Frank sneered. "Oh, you think you're so clever."

Rogers nodded. "I think I am. What man do you want to kill, Grimm?"

Using his name like that was also infuriating. Heat was building under his scalp. Frank pulled a raspy breath through his crooked nose. "You knew before you asked, Rogers. I want to kill that man I blame for it all."

Rogers opened his mouth to respond, but Miguel beat him to it. "It's *you*. *You're* the man you blame, but you can't do it, can you?"

Frank kept himself from looking. Fixed his gaze on a crack on the floor. "No."

Rogers put a hand on Frank's shoulder. Contact that felt like persecution. "Believe it or not. We know how you feel."

Miguel claimed Frank's other shoulder. "Let us help, brother."

The feet of the other participants sounded like pursuit as they gathered around to offer their support. Closing in for the kill.

Rogers' fingers tightened. "A man like you could never do it, though."

"Do what?"

"Kill yourself."

Frank shook his head. "No. It's just not right."

Miguel's fingers tightened. Like they had rehearsed this whole thing. "That's why we go back. Over and over. To put ourselves in the sights. Let God do it, so at least we ain't gotta blame ourselves for that too."

Frank closed his eyes. "I'll be damned. I guess you *do* understand."

Then he shrugged off their hands. Turned away from acceptance he neither wanted nor deserved. But even as he threaded his way through the compressing crowd, Frank knew they would take what had just happened as a positive step.

He hit the loft stairs, hoping his plans would work out.

Frank had no *reason* to hope, but if everything went perfectly, he'd be dead before they asked him to join again anyway.

Chapter Three

FRANK COULD STILL HEAR the voices below him. Over an hour had passed since he stormed off in a huff. Straight to his liquor cabinet.

He stocked it with as many different types and brands as he could. It made him feel like a collector — or even a connoisseur — instead of a lonely man with a problem.

Especially since he never actually sat down to enjoy the nice reposado he had paid forty dollars for. Instead, pouring it into more iced tea. Measuring by eye.

He moved out to the balcony where he could get a sense of how his efforts had made Carmen's grave look. From the ground, it had seemed like a fair match between his trimming and Mo's regular yardwork. From on high, though — he could easily see the ragged edges of his handiwork.

It appeared sparse, rather than tidy. Pitiful and dying. Dirt showing through the patches.

He pushed stringy hair off his forehead, but the breeze folded it back over. It looked a lot like the thin weeds.

Frank noticed cars leaving. Waves and shouts. Mo was

back at the RV with a polishing rag in one hand. A squirt bottle of compound in the other.

Gen came out to him carrying a tray of drinks. Probably some lunch too. It struck him as a scene from childhood. The dutiful wife bringing food to the laboring husband.

Only instead of an apron and pearls, she wore a tank top and tight shorts. Her legs were like trees. Thick neck and shoulders. And her man was black. Something not often seen in the late fifties.

Even from his distant perch, he could see their love for each other. Wondered again how he had ever missed it.

For all of her powerful muscles, she was still a girly-girl. Cutesy. Almost prissy. Mo was even more impressive now that he had stripped the fat to the bulging strength underneath.

For some reason, they just fit together. Frank wasn't sure if it was because he knew them, and in his mind, they were a unit. Or maybe it was just as the world intended, and two people meant for each other had found their ideal mate.

He had thought the same thing about him and Sarah. Especially at the perfect child they had managed to produce.

So maybe he was wrong about them too.

He took advantage of their distraction to go down into the barn and leave by the side exit that would take him down the long edge of the yard.

Under the old carport to the front porch. It had a visible lean. White paint warping off the railing in the humidity. Rocking chairs. Small table. An empty cooler tipped over to drain. A stack of coasters.

The front door was flanked by two wide windows. One had the curtains thrown back to reveal the shadow of the living room. The other had the curtains drawn. Wheat-colored linen.

Frank smelled smoke from the grill before going inside.

He shut the door behind him and paused to let his eyes adjust to the dim interior. Felt a chill ripple through him as the severely cooled air washed over him.

He knew it wasn't for Mo or Gen. They were far more tolerant of the heat than GG. He just couldn't take it anymore.

Frank leaned his head back to rest on the door. Held his breath against the anxiety forming in his chest. He was never ready for it. No longer knew how to prepare.

GG loved all forms of weightlifting. Unlike some of the meatheads back at Stan's gym, he had even loved bodybuilding. Could name hundreds of bodybuilders. From the Golden Era — Arnold Schwarzenegger's heyday — to the current sidewalk-crackers like Phil Heath.

GG held a particular soft spot in his heart for Ronnie Coleman, though. The man he still said was the greatest Mr. Olympia in the history of the sport.

Frank sometimes had trouble with calling it a sport — at least the posing-on-stage portion. That seemed a lot like a testosterone-fueled beauty pageant. The work that was put in at the gym, though? *That* was amazing, and some of these bodybuilders put up numbers that would win power-lifting competitions.

One of Ronnie Coleman's catchphrases was simple. One that GG had often used to pump up the lifters at Wild One.

"Ain't nothing to it, but to do it."

Frank nodded to himself, as if he had said it out loud.

He moved along the wall. Into the kitchen. Turned toward the side yard to look out the window over the sink.

No view except the side of the RV. Some grill smoke rolling up along its roof.

He sighed before turning to the open bedroom door to his right. Tried to force a smile and ended in something like neutrality.

He could see GG's bed. The fuzzy narwhal blanket hanging down the side. The TV hanging from an articulating bracket played a silent Minecraft video.

"Hey, Dad," GG called from inside. "I saw you on the porch through the curtains. You coming on in?"

Frank's face crumpled into grief when he heard GG call him *Dad*. Smoothed his expression back to the previous semblance of normal. Managed a smile as he entered.

"Hey, buddy. How you feeling today?"

GG looked up with a grin that only spread to one side of his face. The other was slack and waxy. The brow dropping almost low enough to cover the eye. A lot like Frank's scarred one.

Where GG had once been a mountain of a man, he was now an oversized skeleton. Bones showing through skin. Dark hollows in the creases of his joints. The chemo had made his head a smooth egg. The surgical scar lacing along the side of his scalp was the color of old blood.

No eyebrows. A few twisted hairs on his chin.

His decline had happened so fast. Like the world changing during the flash of lighting.

A tablet was open on his lap. Another video playing without sound. This one the highlights of some strongman competition.

GG nudged it aside with his withering left hand while motioning to the chair beside his bed with his good hand. "It's a bad one, Dad. But most of 'em are these days. Have a seat."

"Thanks, buddy." Frank looked away from his friend as

he walked around the bed. Sat with a grunt before leaning in to look at the screen on GG's lap. "Whatcha got there?"

He leaned his head back into the pillow. "Robert Oberst tore his bicep."

Frank nodded. Looked at the posters on the opposite wall. *Teen Titans Go!*, with the teenage version of Robin. The Boy Wonder was wearing a tuxedo, singing to an equally formal Cyborg. GG loved that show. So much that Frank was surprised it wasn't on the TV right now.

Next to it was Stan "The Rhino" Efferding. A massive bodybuilder flexing in front of an impossible stack of weights.

Finally, there was a glazed doughnut with pink sprinkles and a cartoon smile. The caption always made him chuckle. *Two in the pink, one in the sprink.*

GG reached to his bedside table. Hooked a bottle of water. Got the straw to his mouth for a slurping drink. Kept it next to him as he turned to Frank with a critical eye. "You look rough, Dad. You been hitting them sprints?"

Frank nodded. "Sure did, buddy. The bleachers over at Mound Park. All the way to the top ten times. Thought I was gonna die."

"You couldn't be so lucky," GG said. "Did you puke?"

"No, but it was close."

"Then do fifteen next time."

"You got it."

GG nodded like something important had been decided. "You up your eggs?"

"I have, yeah. That's a lot of saturated fat, though."

"Building block of testosterone. Besides, eggs got a lot of choline in 'em. The way you drink, you need as much liver protection as you can get."

That didn't make sense to Frank, but he wasn't a

doctor, nor did he plan on living long enough to get heart disease. "Then more eggs it is."

"And the salmon? You gotta get it once a week. And the oranges."

Frank put his hand on GG's arm, even though he wasn't sure if he could feel it. "I'm doing it all, buddy. I promise."

GG pressed his lips together. Breathed through his nose.

A single tube ran along the sheets. To a cannula under his ribs. It delivered morphine, and every time it pumped, Frank was reminded of aquarium bubbles. The sound made him tighten his grip on GG's arm.

GG's eyes opened, then the good one widened in alarm. Like he just remembered something important. "It won't be long now, Dad."

"You got plenty of time, buddy."

"Oh, I don't know if I can make it, Dad."

Frank rubbed his eyes. "I'm so sorry. I wish …"

He trailed off. Listened to the bubbles stop. Waited for GG's breathing to ease.

GG adjusted his position with a grunt. "What do you wish, Dad?"

Frank sighed. "I wish you didn't have to suffer like this."

"Maybe I don't."

"What do you mean?"

GG fumbled with his tablet. Got it flipped over. Then he dug next to his thigh until he found the remote, killed the TV, then dropped the remote back on his sheets. "It's a bad one today, Dad."

Frank looked away as he nodded. "I know."

"I mean … a *bad* one."

Frank stroked GG's wrist. "I was thinking of taking a

trip. One of my weekenders, you know? Down to Rosa Alta."

"That beach with that Ty Kirby dickhead?"

The new studio for *In Our Midst*. Moved since gaining popularity on LiveLyfe.

Frank nodded. "That's right. Just checking some things out. Some loose ends."

"You're almost over it, ain't you?"

"I think so."

GG sniffed. "Then can you do something for me?"

"Of course. Anything you need, buddy."

"Cool, then can you kill me?"

Frank thought of the first time somebody wanted him to do something that made him sick just thinking about it. Freya leaving a note where she knew he'd see it.

My father is raping me. I need you to kill him.

He had balked then, but this time he threw himself back in his chair. GG turned to face him so Frank could see the good eye leaking tears. Anguish pulling his skin tight over angled cheekbones.

"Please," GG gasped. "It hurts so bad. I just want it to stop."

Frank stood on quavering legs. Horror making his jaw fall open.

GG looked away. Slammed his head back into his pillow. "It hurts, Dad. So fucking bad. But the worst part is, I'm losing myself. I'm *forgetting*."

Frank made his way to the foot of the bed. Around to the wall where he kept himself pressed against the paneling. His shoulder tore a corner of the doughnut poster.

"The pain's bad enough, Dad. But imagine dying without knowing who you are."

Frank froze. Stared into GG's desperate gaze. "Imagine *living* without knowing who you are."

GG pointed. "You do it. You hear me?"

Frank shook his head. Walked toward the door. GG lunged up and reached out his clawed hand to grab Frank's upper arm in a crushing grip.

He tried to get away, but GG's old strength was still in reserve. Under all that cancer and suffering. Pain radiated down to his fingers. GG pulled, and Frank couldn't resist.

He was inches away when GG finally released him. Sat still as he stared into his eyes. "If you love me," GG whispered. "If you *ever* loved me, you'll do it."

Frank blinked his tears away. "Buddy, that's not fair."

GG fell back. Looked up at the ceiling. His Adam's apple bobbed as he swallowed. "I know it ain't, Dad. But you know what I learned?"

Frank straightened up. Retreated to the door, but paused before leaving. "What did you learn, buddy?"

"Ain't *nothing* fair."

Frank left the way he came. He was almost running by the time he got back to the barn.

He opened the tequila bottle, but didn't bother pouring it into the tea.

Chapter Four

FRANK HAD trouble thinking about anything else on his way to Rosa Alta. GG's wasted face hanging in his memory. He even tried to distract himself with Ty Kirby's nonsensical podcast, *The Tip of the Iceberg*.

His mind was dominated by fear and anxiety. Pity for GG. Shame in his own inability to fulfill the dying man's wish. Or maybe it was *unwillingness*.

Frank sighed a gust of fresh frustration. Turned up the volume on the Dodge's radio.

He'd spent most of Carmen's money — and most of his time — on the van. Stan had kept it in good shape. It suffered mostly from just sitting. Stains from various bodily fluids during their escape from Playa Dolor.

Steam-cleaning the carpets hadn't worked. So it was all new, along with the replacement seat covers. New folding mechanism for the rear seat so Frank had a bed whenever he was on a stakeout. Similar supplies to what he had carried in his Avalanche.

Plus some extras that might help him with his *new* goals.

Other than new brakes, a tune-up, and fluid changes, the last thing he had installed was a Bluetooth adapter to the old cassette/CD player combo. He'd found an old Van Halen album in the glovebox. Baked yellow from decades of heat. Popped it in, and it had played with the warble of stretched drive belts.

The wave of nostalgia had been overwhelming, even though he'd never really been a David Lee Roth fan. Just the feeling of being in a different era. Back when things were far less complicated.

He rewound the tape back to the start of side one. Put it back in the glovebox. Something about it being there was a comfort.

His phone was paired with the receiver in the dash, and the Livelyfe audio came through the van's speakers loud and clear. *Too* clear for Kirby's voice.

"When you look at the amount of control the media has over our lives, it's no wonder we are losing the minds of our children."

Deep, with even more gravel than it used to have. Processed through studio equipment to make him sound more like the alpha male he always claimed to be.

Frank steered down the road running parallel with the ocean. His last turn until pulling into the parking lot next to the boardwalk at Rosa Alta. Past the golf course clubhouse. The local sports bar/seafood restaurant, The Open Net.

A Sloppy's made to look like a tropical beach house.

"It's in the eyes," Kirby said. "That twinkle that shows the reptilian glint. That cold, emotionless way they have of reporting the news."

Ever since gaining such a following with *In Our Midst*, Kirby had been flirting with mainstream opportunities.

He'd even had several meetings. Imminent deals he had breathlessly reported on his podcast.

Of course, his popularity had been inflated. Fans and follows purchased to give him the social currency required to convince the networks that he was the next big thing.

After Frank had gotten out of Playa Dolor, Kirby's shine had started to dim. Without the state law enforcement support he enjoyed, his show had faded. His views and subscriptions had plummeted. And like every other bottom-of-the-barrel celebrity, he'd turned to more and more desperate measures to regain that sparkle.

He had delved into every conspiracy. Every whack-job theory. From aliens to politics to Bigfoot. This week he was focused on the lizard people and their controlling the flow of information.

Throughout it all, Kirby maintained a position of sympathetic sufferer. One of the little people with the resources and determination to uncover the truth for his fellow man.

As his new popularity grew, so did the burden of his new followers. There was some overlap with his previous pool of fans, but they had mostly transitioned from terrified housewives and crime conspiracy theorists to shameless end-of the-worlders. The kinds of people that had filters that made their urine drinkable. Extra foil in the cupboard in case the aliens tried to control their minds during the inevitable invasion.

Kirby had to be bitter about missing out on the network money, but he was also sure Kirby was doing just fine with LiveLyfe advertising.

Sponsors that peddled inferior earbuds, underwear that kept your testicles in a separate pouch for comfort but were really designed to make your package look larger, manscaping clippers, and a different mobile game every week.

Kirby had recently managed to bag a Hill of Beans spot at the top of his second hour. To some listeners, that was proof of the podcast's quality, but to Frank, it was proof that the jerk's audience was growing enough to make the numbers work. Hill of Beans knew it would gain more customers through Kirby's listeners than it lost to being associated with a scumbag.

An odd sort of proof of a lot of what Kirby maintained in many of his rants. Americans were worth only as much as the cash they could hand over to the corporations, and the data they could give to the government.

Information was now worth more than oil.

But none of that bothered Frank. He only had to look at the pictures of his daughter's crime scene to understand the world's cruelty.

Frank was angry that Kirby no longer saw him as worthy content. Framing him as the rapist and murderer of his own daughter just wasn't worth the clicks anymore. And the speed at which Frank and Stan had gone from monsters to old news was staggering.

It *did* mean they were under less public scrutiny. But it also meant the police — at least the ones implicated in the activity at Pedophile Junction — were looking even harder.

So far, Frank had continued to escape their notice. But that was soon coming to an end.

He pulled the van into a spot that always seemed empty. Right next to the chain link corral that hid the dumpsters. Trash that barely smelled worse than the aroma floating over from Sloppy's. A swirl of flies. Bees looking for the sugar in the melting snow cones and milkshakes.

He kept the passenger side close to the fence. Just an

inch or two from the mirror's edge. Lowered the volume before rolling the window down.

Killed the engine and leaned the seat back to a more comfortable angle.

As Kirby signed off for a mid-show break, Frank pulled the small cooler up from behind him. Cracked it open to get at the egg salad sandwiches. Half a bag of teriyaki beef jerky. Two pomegranate vodka seltzers. Gallon of water.

Settled back to wait. Watched the yellow stucco building across the street through the driver's side mirror.

A LiveLyfe ad played. Frank never understood a plat-form advertising *for* the platform he was listening on, but maybe pirated content was a bigger problem than he thought. He chalked up his five-dollar-a-month subscrip-tion fee to *research*, but if the podcast was going to be stolen, they might as well let the thieves know where it came from.

Two minutes into the quarter-hour break, Kirby was outside, the cigarette hanging from his lips likely lit before he opened the door. A trail of smoke swirled behind him like the wake of a tugboat.

Kirby walked to the cover of the fluttering red umbrella at the edge of the concrete pad he used as a break area. One hand holding the cigarette. The other with a phone held to the side of his head.

Frank wasn't interested in the conversation. Only in what he hoped was to follow.

At that thought, he heard a car door. The sound of feet crunching across scattered sand. A figure appeared in the mirror. A man's back. Casual slacks. Sport coat pulling back as he checked a pistol holstered in the small of his back.

The cop walked straight to Kirby.

Frank sat forward to watch. Chewed as quietly as he

could, even though there was no way he could hear what was being said.

Kirby glanced up and saw the cop's approach. Signed off of the call and plastered on a greasy grin. Held the cigarette away from his face as he stepped forward with his hand extended.

The cop shook it, then followed Kirby to a picnic table where he put one foot up on the far bench. Frank could finally see the man's face. Didn't bother taking a picture. He was good at remembering faces. When he found out what the cop's name was, *then* he'd write it down.

He only knew it was a *different* face. Not from any he recognized from the lists he and Stan had amassed while hiding in the dark of Heirloom Antiques. Like many of the faces Frank had seen hanging around, the cop looked like some new blood installed after an official culling. Out with the old, and all that.

The only problem was the new team was as bad as the old one. He couldn't even trust the deputies in the sheriff's office where he used to work. And those at the top were still there. The powerful never let go of their power without a fight. Frank knew he had no chance at getting justice up the ladder. He'd have to stick with the scumbags down at *his* level.

Kirby looked down at his watch. Lit another cigarette with the butt of the last one. Dropped it on the ground and mashed it with a boot heel. Thick soles to make him look taller.

Frank felt the wisps of his own hair itching the side of his face and had to admit, Kirby's transplants looked good.

Kirby and the cop chatted like old friends, Kirby clearly acting like a subordinate, eager to impress his superior. It was also obvious that Kirby couldn't tell that the cop seemed to genuinely like him. Which explained why Kirby kept trying so hard.

Frank snorted in disgust. Drained his first seltzer. Chased it down with a third of his water.

Wiped his eyes while catching his breath. Unwrapped a fresh sandwich as Kirby and the cop shook hands again, then parted ways.

Kirby puffed on his cigarette all the way back to the door. Made a token attempt to blow the smoke over his shoulder before rushing inside.

The cop went back to his car, and when he pulled out, Frank made note of the make and model. A Gray Ford Escape. A little SUV that looked like a cinder block with rounded corners.

Kirby opened the last hour of his podcast with a live read for Justice VPN, and Frank clicked off the radio to eat the rest of his lunch in silence.

He brushed his hands off. Rolled his window back up. Locked the van behind him. After a visit to the blue portable toilet in the brown field behind Kirby's studio, he walked back to pause at the picnic table Kirby and the cop had taken their break at.

Frank had learned about Rosa Alta from Kirby's own podcast intro. "Coming to you live from the Watchtower in sunny Rosa Alta, it's the *Tip of the Iceberg* podcast, with your leader of the modern rational revolution, Ty Kirby." Frank still cringed when he heard it.

He had made notes of any official information but had really only come up with a P.O. box address always mentioned at the bottom of the first hour. He could only imagine the kind of things Ty Kirby's listeners were sending him.

The website for the podcast was no help. Generic pictures of the town, but none of the building the studio was in. Frank had begun to wonder if it was even a real place, or if he would find Ty Kirby in a basement somewhere. Shouting up through the ceiling for his mom to bring him more soup.

The post office had been easy to find, though. Like the rest of the town, the official buildings seemed in desperate need of an update. Stuck in the 70s, but with modern signage. Antennas and satellite dishes. The crowd of newer buildings all around. There was something unsettling about it to Frank. Like an old woman trying to look young again in spite of her obvious decline. He was pretty sure Jimmy Buffett had a song about somebody like that.

When he had gone inside, Frank was pleased to see a bored twenty-something behind the counter instead of a seen-it-all veteran looking at another five years before retirement. A young man clearly watching the clock barely looked up when the bell over the door clanged. Echoed through a dark lobby full of ornate cubbies locked up with corroded brass hardware.

Frank gave a smile that wasn't returned. On top of a crisp one-hundred-dollar bill, he placed the note on which he had written Kirby's P.O. box number. Slid it slowly across while watching the kid's expression go from boredom to interest the closer the money got to the other side of the counter. "I'd like the info on this boxholder, please."

The kid's gaze flickered up to meet his. Back down to the money. As soon as Frank removed his finger the kid shrugged. Snatched the bribe from the counter. "One moment, sir."

It sounded like the first time he had *ever* said "sir."

Frank was envious of the kid's speed on the keyboard. Then the kid leaned over a small notepad. Scrawled in lazy script. Passed his note along with Frank's — minus the hundo — and leaned back with a genuine smile that transformed his face. He was suddenly too handsome for the post office. "Will there be anything else, sir?"

Frank smiled in return. "I'm good." When he looked back through the glass of the front door as he left, the kid was still smiling.

It had taken a small effort to decipher the kid's handwriting, but it had led him to Alta Drive. To a two-story building that looked like a Saltines box standing on its end. Flaking gray stucco. A dirty rectangle over the entry door where the old business sign used to be. It was attached to an entire block of two-story shops built to look like a strip of Mexican pueblos. *Watchtower* was a bit of a stretch, but it was certainly better than any description of the actual building.

After nestling into his spot next to the garbage, Frank had begun to learn Kirby's habits. There almost every day, but he only recorded on Fridays. He had many visitors throughout the week, but the same few came during his smoke breaks during show days. He was up to almost a pack a day — no wonder his voice sounded so rough — and he had lost a terrible amount of weight. Frank hadn't bothered trying to find out why. There was something else much more interesting.

Many nights through the week, Kirby would stay in the Watchtower well into the night, but no lights shone from any of his windows. Instead, lights on the second floor of the shops next door came on. Just bleeding around the edges of the drapes. He was very curious about what was going on up there.

Frank glanced over at the door Kirby used to get out to the patio. Noted the security camera by the door pointed toward the front sidewalk. Reached into his pocket as he ducked under the flapping edge of the picnic table umbrella. Pulled out the small recorder. Dropped into a squat that drove stretching pain into his thighs. It took only moments to drive the two tiny screws that held the small device in place, but it felt like an hour. Even sitting in a breeze under the shade of the table, Frank felt the sweat pouring down his sides.

He'd give it a week before coming back to get it. Hopefully, there would be something on there he could use.

He almost brained himself on the edge of the table when he jumped up to brush his hands off. Looked back at the door before heading back to the van. He worried that Kirby might come out. Or that the cop would return. But even if either of them did, thanks to Owens, Frank was certain they wouldn't recognize him.

His newfound anonymity came with the development of a snoring problem, but he lived alone in a barn. Nobody but himself to disturb, and he could drink himself to sleep most nights.

Though, come to think of it, *that* might be why he snored so bad.

Frank chuckled to himself as he opened the rear doors of the van. Grabbed his towel and wide-brimmed straw hat. He had driven all this way. Might as well enjoy the beach since he was here. Sometimes it was difficult in his isolation. In spite of how much he wanted to be alone, he yearned for better company. Just hearing the sounds of other people around him was often enough.

On his way out to find a spot on the sand, he looked back over his shoulder. A string of small shops to Kirby's studio. Souvenirs, frozen yogurt, and a used bookstore.

The second floor above the row of shops, running the span of the entire block. Remembering the lights coming on upstairs, and thinking of the number of cops that seemed to come around all the time, made Frank wonder if this was the tentative location for the next Pedophile Junction franchise.

Owens seemed to be laying low for now, and the cops he'd pressured to quit with his framing of Malick Briar for Rory Day's murder were getting bolder. Perhaps ready for version 2.0.

If he succeeded, a fresh batch of victims were already being lined up somewhere else. Frank understood how little impact he was having on the larger problem of statewide corruption leading to an entire *trade* of underage sex trafficking. Still, he was going to have that impact.

Or die trying. Maybe *and* die trying.

An important conjunction choice, this near the end.

Chapter Five

THE LONG WEEKEND helped Frank forget about GG's haunting request. Listening to hours of Kirby's podcast. Swimming and lying out in the sun.

Cuban food and icy cold beer.

Nobody seemed to mind his van parked by the dumpsters all day, but he hadn't felt comfortable stretching his luck at night. Every town had a Walmart, though. Twenty-four-hour parking and plenty of lights to discourage looky-loos.

A few Saturday hours had been spent at the Rose County Clerk's office. He was looking for publicly available information, but the minute he got to the old building, he knew he was in for a struggle. There were three ways it could have gone. Modern and shiny where everything had been digitized and stored on some cloud system that Frank would have had no chance navigating, old and dusty rows of moldy boxes, or a smooth and pleasant experience with a helpful and polite staff.

He landed right on the middle option.

The interior smelled like stale pipe smoke and sausage

that was on the verge of turning. Ornate carpets worn to a homogenous color the exact shade of the inside of a colon. Dark paneling and old incandescent lighting. It was like he had stepped onto the set of *The Rockford Files*. He expected to look behind him to see a gold Pontiac Firebird in the parking lot.

The burly gentleman sitting behind a tall counter on the left side of the lobby looked like Wilford Brimley's much bigger brother. He was staring at a small CRT television through thick glasses. An open bag of Oreos to his right. A sixty-four-ounce cup from Circle K on his left. The name plate at the edge of the counter was stained melamine. *Monty Henderson*.

Frank was positive that Mr. Henderson checked his sugar, and he checked it often. Had oatmeal in the morning because it was the right thing to do, and the right way to do it. Frank got to the desk before he could think of any more of Wilford's catchphrases. He grinned and waved. "Good morning, sir."

Monty looked up from his TV. Wiped crumbs from his drooping mustache. "Yup."

Frank nodded. Kept his grin nice and wide. Held by the man's stare, he became aware of just how much he had come to resemble a drug-fueled vagrant. "I wonder if you can help me?"

"You're in the wrong place," Monty said. "Didn't you read the sign on the door?"

Frank flushed as he admitted that he hadn't. "I'm not really familiar with this town. Just in for some research and swimming."

"Yup."

Frank waited for more, but Monty seemed to be done for the moment. Frank lifted a finger to point at the ceiling. "This is the Rose County Clerk of Courts building, right?"

"Yup."

"And I assume you are the clerk, or are employed by said entity?"

The right corner of Monty's lips trembled in a smile, making the mustache flutter. "Yup."

Frank nodded like he had learned an amazing fact about the history of the building. Like a tour guide had told him the foundation was made out of petrified bathing suits dug out of the landfill. "So then, there are records kept here?"

"Yup."

"And a search of these records can be performed after paying a fee?"

Monty leaned back and crossed his arms, and his smile widened to make his mustache flare out like butterfly wings. "That's right."

The new response made Frank feel like he was making progress. "Well, since I need to do a search, and it is something this building provides, I fail to see how I am in the wrong place."

Monty's smile became a grin that showed his bottom row of brown teeth. He pointed past Frank's shoulder. "Maybe you should have read the sign."

Frank glanced back at the front door. Back to Monty. "You're going to make me go out there and read it, aren't you?"

"Yup."

Frank maintained his smile until he turned around. Then it became clenched teeth anger. At the door, he smoothed his face, turned to give Monty a big Forest Gump wave, leaned out to read the many bits of paper taped to the inside of the glass. Found the one in question.

This facility is moving to the new government complex in Enola. Closed for official inquiries only. Please go to RoseCoClCo.gov to schedule a records search, or use the online search feature. (search results subject to the completion of Rose County's record digitization efforts)

The "r" and "t" in *efforts* had been transposed, scribbled out with a black marker, and corrected with a red marker.

Frank spread his hands and nodded sheepishly as he turned back to look at Monty. Still sitting with his arms crossed and eyes twinkling. When Frank got back to the counter, Monty watched him with raised eyebrows. Frank knew he would have to be careful.

Or increase the amount he was willing to offer as a bribe.

"How long you been here, Mr. Henderson?"

"Call me Monty," he said. Then he looked at his watch. "Since six this morning."

Frank suppressed a growl of frustration. "Thank you, Monty. But I expect you know what I'm asking."

Monty grinned. "Yup."

Frank thought he was going to make him ask again. Then Monty dug into the crinkling bag for a fresh cookie. "Forty years."

Frank whistled in appreciation. "If you don't mind me asking, why haven't you retired? It's been pretty good for *me* so far." The lie almost stuck in Frank's throat.

Monty crunched on the Oreo, sending black powder to cascade down into his dirty white beard. He shrugged with a sigh. "It's just me at home now. I can spend my day here alone just as easy as anywhere else.

Frank sensed an opening. "I know how you feel. After my wife died, I just couldn't be in that house anymore." He hoped he had guessed correctly, and the thousand dollars he had ready in his pocket could stay there. "It just felt …" He paused as if he was searching for words.

36

"Colorless," Monty whispered.

Frank had expected *empty* or *lonely*, but the word Monty used took his breath away. A word so apt he was surprised he had never used it himself. He looked away with a nod of understanding. "Exactly."

"How did she pass?" Monty asked. His voice was soft and rough. All the mirth replaced by weight.

Frank kept his gaze focused on the counter. "Breast cancer. A few years now. We had planned to buy some shops here out on Alta Drive. Up above the little stores along the beach. But it looks like somebody beat us to it." He laughed. "Well, the cancer ended our plans before that."

Monty puffed out a breath like he was trying to blow out a candle. "We were gonna go down to Key West. A condo out by the aquarium. But she had a stroke."

"I'm so sorry," Frank said.

Monty nodded. Then he looked at Frank in confusion. "I don't understand."

Frank wanted to offer the man a hug. Then he thought of how he had rejected the therapy circle. Some people didn't want comfort. He just had to find out what Monty wanted. He sighed. "Me and Sarah used to look at blueprints. Like we were going to build something special whenever we finally decided on something to buy. Something to spend our time doing. Together. For the rest of our lives."

He didn't have to fake the emotion in his voice.

Monty sucked air through his teeth. "You got an address?"

Frank produced the scrap of paper on which he had scribbled the addresses of the upper floors next to Ty Kirby's Watchtower. Monty took it and turned to an ancient computer that had aged into the color of stretched caramel. The keyboard sounded like rattling bones.

Monty looked at the paper through his lenses. At the screen over the top of the frames. He nodded to himself. "B-17," he muttered.

"Bingo," Frank said.

Monty chuckled as he heaved himself out of his seat. He wore suspenders *and* a belt. He hustled off without asking Frank to follow, but Frank rushed after him anyway.

"We're already two years into this project," Monty said. "The way the government spends money, you'd think they could get it done quicker. I think they just don't know what to do with all the old stuff."

"Like you?" Frank asked.

Monty grinned as they turned into a short hallway that led to a wide set of descending stairs. "Don't *nobody* know what to do with me."

The bottom of the stairs opened into a deep room filled with long open shelves. The walls were lined with cabinets that were nearly as tall as the ceiling. Frank estimated it was at least ten feet high.

"This is the print room," Monty said, grunting down the last few steps. "Back to sixty-seven or so, all the way up to oh six when they started filing 'em in CAD or some such. Digital nonsense."

He struck Frank as the kind of guy that called it the *Interwebs.* Monty consulted his paper, turned down a row, waddled all the way to the end. The shelf he stopped at held wide trays full of drawings. He thumbed up through the stack, stopping next to a flag hanging out. The number 17 on it. He slid the top one out. Took a quick look. Shook his head before moving to the next one down.

"That one was drainage. Shared by neighboring buildings. That God-awful Mexican restaurant around the corner."

After a few more, he found one that satisfied him. Carried it out into better light. "This one was from a permit request back in ninety-nine. Some electrical updates, but it shows the dimensioned structure. Will that do?"

Frank nodded. "That'll do just fine."

Monty grinned as he rolled the drawing into a tube. "I gotta rubber band up front."

As Frank moved to follow, he asked, "Won't this be missed?"

Monty threw his head back and laughed. "About as much as I will after I'm gone."

By the time they got back to the counter in the lobby, Monty was red-faced and out of breath. "Whew," he exclaimed as he dropped back into his chair. "Looks like I got *my* exercise for the day."

Monty snapped a rubber band on the end of the tube. Rolled it down to the middle and held it out for Frank. Frank took it with his left and extended his right. "The name's Frank, by the way."

Idiot old man. Using his real name again.

Monty nodded as he shook hands. Then he settled back for another Oreo.

Frank pointed at the computer. "That thing wouldn't happen to say who bought it, would it?"

Monty leaned forward. Pulled his glasses down out of the way to see the screen. "Huh," he said in surprise. "That Ty Kirby guy. Cora used to watch his show on the LiveLyfe. The one about monsters or some such."

"I heard he died," Frank said.

"It happens."

Frank paused before saying goodbye. "Why don't you go on down there?"

"Down where?"

"To Key West. Lock the doors and just go. Don't spend it alone, Monty. Go where there's life. Where there's *color*."

Monty nodded as he looked away. "I just might do that, Frank. I just might."

Frank saluted with the blueprint tube. Turned and left in silence. He knew Monty wasn't a *just do it* kind of guy.

Chapter Six

Most of Sunday was spent on the beach in front of the Watchtower. Frank hooked his Chromebook up to the wifi signal of his cellphone, and it only took him three tries. It had been easier when Stan was around to handle that kind of thing. It only cost Frank a few minutes of being made fun of for being an out-of-touch old man. With a little practice, he could now do both. The technical stuff *and* calling himself old.

His gut tightened with loneliness. He drowned it with a beer warming in the sun.

He started with a simple real estate search of the address. Found several listings aggregated over many different sites. Pieced together the building's history from some of the older descriptions. Coupled with the blueprints, he was able to get a decent picture of the interior.

It had been separate units at one time. Each one directly over one of the units on the lower floor. Sometime in the eighties, it had been purchased by an investment firm from Texas. They had built a new unit on the end that had started life as a pet store. The lease changed hands over the next decades, but the top floors never went anywhere.

They had been converted into one single unit of five rooms connected by a single hallway that connected them all. The front entry of what would eventually become the Watchtower led to a common reception area upstairs. The hallway ran parallel with the storefront to end at an alcove that shared a wall with the building on the corner. A metal door emptied into a fire escape that was in serious need of some maintenance. Dumped into the alley behind that was lined with a chain link laced with brown vines and plastic strips as a wind break.

The logistics of renewing such a space were probably beyond the courage of many investors, and thus the place had stayed vacant for years. Frank speculated about how and why it had finally been sold.

Perhaps Ty Kirby had come into some *real* money. A contract with some bad people to keep his mouth shut. Easier to pay than to silence.

Had he bought it as a place where Pedophile Junction could resume? His offering to the group in exchange for his membership? Or maybe the cops had pressured him into surrendering. Or maybe they had fronted the money as long as he put his name on the papers.

None of that was enough to lead him directly to Owens, but it opened a couple doors. He just had to decide which one to walk through first.

He rotated around in the sand to look up at the building over the roof of his van. Five high windows spaced evenly apart but shifted toward the corner to line up with the entry doors of the shops on the bottom floor. That meant they weren't directly in front of the interior doors.

Even if he had a vantage point, he wouldn't be able to see inside any of the rooms. He would have to get a little closer.

Frank closed his Chromebook. Finished another beer he didn't remember opening. Gathered up everything he had scattered around his little spot of claimed beach territory. Almost forgot his flip flops.

Dumped it all in the van. Slipped his multi-tool and lockpick set into his cargo pocket. He jogged across the street. To the patio next to the Watchtower. The colorful umbrellas on the picnic tables were no longer a mystery. The most recent business to occupy this space was an Inside Scoop, and if there was ever another reason to hate Ty Kirby, Frank had found it.

The memory of the ice cream parlor he had taken Jenny to every week flashed through his mind. Then he remembered punching Patrick Dahl in the face over a bowl. Both great memories in their own way. Both ruined by the association with Ty Kirby.

He walked without looking around. Kept his shoulders as straight as he could. Held his head up. Made sure his smile was slight, and not nervous or eager. He didn't want to look like somebody creeping along, *trying* not to be noticed.

Frank was just a guy cutting through the alley. Nothing to see here.

He continued down to where the line of shops met the large corner building. To a rectangle of shadow next to a yellow metal door. The rear at this end was shielded by the chain link barrier. A long shadow cast by the fence met the black at the recess.

Frank ducked into it and put his back against the wall.

Glanced back the way he had come to make sure he hadn't been noticed.

Not a soul. Just the sound of the music from the shops. Activity from the beach. Passing cars.

The old metal stairs hung from bolts barely holding in the brick. A ladder descended at an angle from the bottom landing. He reached up and tested his weight on it. A sagging vibration, but it held as he climbed. Through to the bottom landing, then onto the stairs. Staying on the inside of each step until he reached the top.

The door at the top was a featureless metal slab. A thumb latch under a keyed lock. It was out of sight of the front sidewalks and parking spaces. Blocked by a facade that extended up like the face of a Hollywood set.

For a few moments, Frank would be in clear view of traffic at the edge of the building at the other end down from the corner. People on the beach at the very edge of the water.

But how many passersby would even know he wasn't supposed to be there? It only took one … the *wrong* one. Like one of the cops coming by for a visit. Or Ty Kirby himself.

He tried the pitted handle, but it held solid. He fished out the lockpick and hoped for the best. He had never been very good at picking locks. Stan was a whiz. Frank was the tortoise to Stan's hare. He was soon sweating. It dripped from the end of his nose to make ringing splats against the metal grating under his feet.

Finally, he felt it tumble over. Resisted the urge to look around with wide eyes to reassure himself he was still unobserved. He put the set back in his pocket. Pushed the handle while holding the door closed. Breathed a sigh of relief when it depressed with a rusty pop. He released the handle. Made sure the door remained shut. There was no way he was going to enter. He knew nothing about the existence or status of alarms. Hadn't been watching closely enough to know if anybody was inside.

He just wanted to see if the door stayed unlocked. He couldn't imagine Ty Kirby — or any of his rapist buddies — leaving by the fire escape unless there was a raid. Or an actual *fire*. He would check back in a week when he retrieved his recorder.

He crept back down to the alley where the air felt cooler. Easier to breathe. He wiped the sweat off his face. Thought about the dinner and drinks he was going to treat himself with. He had to celebrate these little victories. He was lost in patting himself on the back when he stepped around the corner of the Watchtower. Out of the shadow of the alley and into the sun of the patio. Right into Ty Kirby's view.

He looked up from where he sat at the table. Right into Frank's eyes. Blew smoke up into a cloud that hung inside the umbrella.

Frank stumbled to a halt. If there was *anyone* that knew his face, it was Ty Kirby. He had transmitted photos of him for years while trying to frame him for multiple rapes and murders on his disgusting show.

But there was no recognition. Ty only shook his head. Lifted his shoulders in a question as he took another drag from his cigarette and pulled his phone away from his ear. "Can I help you?"

He didn't sound very helpful.

Frank shook his head numbly. Then took a step. Bit down on the rage boiling up in his chest. Filling him so it was hard to breathe. Then he pointed at Kirby's heart. Forced himself to smile instead of snarl. "Can I get one of those?"

Kirby's face became pained annoyance. He rolled his

eyes. "Yeah, sure." He hung the cigarette from the corner of his mouth. Reached around to the table behind him. Pulled the pack up and shook one loose. "I'm on fucking hold," he growled.

Frank barely kept himself from lunging over and choking the bastard. Instead taking the cigarette between shaking fingers. When Kirby struck his lighter, Frank almost bent to put his mustache in the flame. He'd never smoked before, but he had seen it enough to get the gist of how it worked. Puffed until the flame blossomed on the end, then stood up to take a delicate puff.

It tasted the way a sinus infection felt.

He blew smoke up into the air, then he pointed the cigarette at Kirby's face. "Hey, aren't you that guy? That Ty Kirby guy?"

Kirby grinned. Sat a little straighter. "That's right. You a fan of the show?"

Frank flapped the cigarette at him before pretending to take another puff. "Nah. Rush Limbaugh is *way* better."

Kirby pulled the phone from his ear as his face went from obsequious charm to offended in an eyeblink. "Well fuck *you*, buddy!"

Frank stepped toward the street. Threw his hands out. "Hey man, relax."

Kirby stood from the table. "No, *you* fucking relax!"

"Okay, okay. *Sorry*."

Kirby sent a distracted look at his phone. Pulled it up to his ear. "What? No, I'm here. Just some asshole outside the studio."

Frank drew in a deep breath. "Asshole? Well, fuck *you*, buddy!" Then he laughed at the scandalized look on Kirby's face. He could tell the man wanted to charge him. Was torn between petty revenge and the phone call.

As Stan had often told him, there was often an appropriate time for inappropriate language. Out of all the times Frank had forced himself to use it, this had been the most satisfying.

He walked back to the beach without going past his van. He didn't want Kirby seeing what he drove.

Chapter Seven

A NICE HEAVY meal of Sloppy's on the way home, and Frank found himself regretting every bite as he worked each one off at Mound Park Monday morning.

That's also when GG came rushing to the forefront of his mind. Demanding and distracting.

It was cooler than usual. Clouds across the sky. A stiff breeze making the American flag snap on the pole.

Frank took his small cooler all the way to the top of the bleachers. Three tiers high that felt like a mountaintop.

He opened the cooler to fish out three cold bottles of Corona, the little seven-and-a-half-ounce ones he usually tipped upside down into a margarita. Then he set an opener next to them before taking his time back down to the bottom.

Three rounds of five would give him the fifteen that GG had prescribed. One beer during each rest. A small reward to keep himself going.

He took his time warming up and getting loose. He didn't care about injury sidelining his fitness efforts — if the word *fitness* still applied to what he was doing. Using beer as an incentive for bleacher sprints. He was worried about injury knocking him off the track of his investigation — if *investigation* was the right word.

Revenge was probably better. He'd even take *spite*.

Either way, Frank had to make sure he was ready for the effort. Forty-five minutes of warmup for five minutes of furious effort. Not counting the drinking part.

Frank was sweating once he was finally ready. Heart rate already climbing. He stood at the bottom to look up in near despair. It seemed so far to the top. He imagined GG giving him the *start* signal, and he hit it. Feet clanging off the aluminum bleachers as he put in a pretty respectable performance. All the way to the fifth rep, to finally collapse at the top.

That little beer was so cold in his hands, if he'd had the breath, he would have gasped in pleasure. He opened it, then drank every drop with his heartbeat pounding in his neck.

It was hard getting back to the bottom. Every step felt like the impact raced straight up his spine. He'd barely caught his breath before the round-two alarm went off on his phone.

The second beer felt colder than the first, even though it had been out of the cooler for longer. His head throbbed. A stitch in his side.

His foot hit the clay track right as the third alarm rang out. With GG yelling at him in his mind to *push*. His final sprint was more of a desperate hobbling climb.

He had to carry the last beer down before opening it. Sit next to his bag and towel with his head hanging. Elbows on his thighs with the beer dangling between his knees. For a few minutes, he thought GG was going to get what he wanted, but the desire to throw up passed, and he was finally able to enjoy his third bottle.

He dropped the empty in the cooler next to the others. Thought about how much that had hurt. How difficult it had been. Then he thought about GG's pain. Thought about his daughter shouting for help. Screaming in agony.

Rory Day dying in the mud.

Freya looking up to see her father, entering her bedroom in the dead of night.

Frank's broken face couldn't compare. His *suffering* while running up and down the bleachers. Even the pain of losing his wife and daughter wasn't the same as what those little girls had endured.

So much pain in all the world. How could he have ever hoped to do anything about it?

Frank sighed as he pulled out his towel and journal. Noted his metrics in the columns knowing GG would check. His estimate to set the timer had been spot on. GG would probably narrow it for next time. Or add another set of five. Frank had some catching up to do if he was going to get a whole gallon of water in, but the beer had to settle first.

He flipped to the back of the journal. Rotated the whole thing over so the last page was now the first. Started a row of new notes. Crooked columns with scribbled headings. *Name, Occupation, Location,* and *Times.* Once he got the recordings back, he would use any names he might hear in an internet search. Match an online image with his memory, and maybe have a list of suspects.

Then he could catch them. Then he could kill them. Go through as many of them as he needed to get to Owens. His plan was for them to regret every bad decision each one had ever made. A message sent to Owens and those that supported him. Anyone protecting him. Or hiding him.

Frank would make it known that he was willing to

make everyone pay. Promise them that he would release every bit of evidence gathered. Unless they were willing to cut Owens loose.

Once on his own, Owens would come right to him. Remove the thorn from the lion's paw, and the lion would welcome him back, but Frank wouldn't let that happen.

He closed the journal with a snap. Gathered his belongings. Paused to wipe up the sweat that had dripped on the seat. Probably wouldn't have mattered, but it was humid, and the sun wasn't out.

Better to clean the messes you caused than have somebody stumble upon them later.

Advice he could have used months ago.

He didn't think Stan blamed him for what happened in Playa Dolor. Though they had argued about it at the time, he hadn't had the opportunity to ask after the fact. He believed Stan was still alive — Mo would at least tell him if *that* happened. He wanted to talk to his cousin. Go into the kitchen to make a pile of sandwiches and look back to find him watching, ready to complain about how Frank could put more effort into them.

"You gotta learn to make that sandwich *righteous*," he would say.

Stan wasn't *just* a quantity guy, he also saved room for quality. A narrow selection of foods that needed to be just right. Fast food didn't matter. Just serve it in a bucket. Most desserts were the same way.

They had gone to a Burger King once, and Stan had ordered a large chocolate shake. When it was served, Stan had looked back at him with wounded incredulity. The cup was the size of a *medium* soft drink. Not the large. He had questioned the walking pimple behind the cash register, only to be informed that he *had* received a large milkshake. Sizing was different for different beverages.

Stan had clearly thought that was *all* the bullshit, but he held it together. "I tell you what," Stan said. "I'll order *two* larges, and you can just pour 'em both into the *other* large cup. How about it?"

The pimple looked like he was having trouble with that concept. "I'm sorry, sir. That's the size it is."

Stan nodded. "Fine. I want to order another large chocolate shake, but I *also* want a large Dr. Pepper."

At first, Frank had been confused too, but then he realized the soda machine was a self-serve job by the napkins and ketchup pump. When the pimple brought the second shake and the big empty cup for Stan to fill, Stan pulled the lids from both milkshakes. Dumped them in until the large soda cup was filled to the top. Drove the straw in like he was trying to stab the counter through the bottom. Looked up with a triumphant grin. Left the two smaller cups with an inch or so of milkshake in them. Waved with his three bags of food as he walked out.

Frank and the pimple had stared at each other for a moment, then the pimple shrugged. "Welcome to Burger King. Can I take your order?"

The cups were still sitting there when Frank left.

He didn't know what it was about Stan's past that made him pick and choose his gluttony like that. And even with the foods he took care and pride in the preparation of — he still stuffed himself. But the steaks that were distending his belly were expensive, and cooked perfectly. Seasoned just so. Plated to rest. Savored.

Frank wanted to sit across from him again. Argue about food and words. Cry into his shoulder. Feel him pound out that calming rhythm on his back.

He wanted to hear someone stirring in the house when he woke up. He wanted to turn the corner going into his living room and see someone on the couch doing a crossword. Or watching TV. To see them look up and smile. Smell bacon cooking as he woke up. Hear someone curse in the night when they caught their toe on the footstool going to the bathroom in the dark. He wanted to smile at the expectation when he heard someone else's car pull in. Get a teasing message on his phone. Find a note on the fridge.

He wanted to be able to smell chicken marsala without bursting into tears.

He wanted a life that wasn't so damn gray and ugly.

He wanted a little *color*.

Or nothing at all.

Chapter Eight

INSTEAD OF REPORTING straight to GG, Frank went back to the barn so he could start work on the van. But even as he got involved in the details, he couldn't help looking out the wide barn doors.

It was GG's weekly visit to the doctor. Mo and Gen hadn't come out yet. Frank looked at his watch each time, then laughed at himself. He didn't know when the appointment was, so checking the time didn't tell him whether or not they were late.

But he couldn't stop looking.

Knowing GG was still home made him feel watched. Like judgement was coming.

He opened the two side doors on the Dodge. Then the rear doors so the breeze would blow through the interior. He wrestled with the middle seats. Got them released from the pedestals so he could climb in and remove the rear one.

New carpet and front seat covers were a painful contrast to the old fabric remaining on the rest of the seats. Not in *bad* shape, just old and faded. For some reason, every time Frank looked back through the rearview mirror, they seemed to get even shabbier.

They needed an update to match.

He had the seat up on the bench and stripped when GG finally came outside in his wheelchair, with Gen at the handles behind him. His face was a glowing moon under the thin beanie covering his scalp. Pink T-shirt. Fuzzy blanket covering his legs.

Mo's skin was like shiny coal in the bright sunshine.

Frank heard the sound of closing car doors. The engine firing up. He couldn't see them drive away, but he stood there until the sound faded into dull noise from the distant highway.

He turned back to his project with a sigh. Without the silent stare he always felt coming from the house, he could finally relax. Add a tequila on the rocks and he was threatening himself with a nice afternoon.

For the hundredth time, Frank wondered why it was so important. This need to finish a van that was only his because it had been abandoned by the rightful owner. One he would have to make fake papers for come Stan's birthday in March.

He just wanted everything to feel new. After these seats, he would be down to the curtains. But then there was always the dash and the door panels. Maybe they would just need a deep cleaning.

Frank finished recovering the first seat. Leaned against the bench with ice tinkling in the bottom of his empty glass. Looked at the light sparkling off of the van windows.

Maybe it was because that van was kind of like *him*. Maybe too old for what it had been designed for. Faded, but still capable. A few dings and dents. Pitted chrome. Speckles of rust on the rocker panels.

He poured another three fingers before turning to the second seat.

There was no hope left for him. No way to revitalize his existence. Tack a new panel here. Scrape the corrosion away there.

He was at the age where an injury — even a fairly mild one — had life-altering repercussions. A broken hip could heal, but it compromised the rest of the body. Entropy was the real killer of man.

A twenty-year-old falls out of a plane. Shatters most of his body. Heals and comes back stronger than ever. Some aches and pains when the weather turns.

A sixty-year-old sustains the same injuries? He's a goner.

A person gets old enough, just pulling a muscle leads to the end.

A thirty-year-old dies in her sleep, and the family leaves no stone unturned in their quest to find out *why*.

A seventy-year-old dies in her sleep, and everybody shrugs. Must have been her time.

"I'm sorry, but Grammy died of a bad case of natural causes."

The old Dodge Van was something that could be on the road *decades* after he was gone. With enough money and effort, it could be a century if well maintained in a garage. Driven on Sundays until the insurance grew too expensive.

Even a worthless van like this could become priceless with the passage of enough time.

But he would get pneumonia. Break a collarbone. Skin cancer. He couldn't just replace his parts whenever he needed a new one. Until the only original thing left was his brain.

Frank finished the second seat. Set it aside with the

other one. Looked down at his glass to discover somebody had finished while he wasn't paying attention.

Even as he chided himself for drinking too much too early, he chuckled while pouring another.

He looked up at the sound of a vehicle approaching. No idea if it had been long enough for Mo and Gen to be home.

The engine slowed. Came to a stop. Then revved up again.

A white block of a mail carrier's vehicle came into view. The tiny truck accelerated to the next mailbox a couple hundred yards down the road.

Frank took the interruption as an opportunity to break. Set his drink aside. Maybe eat a little something before hitting the booze again.

Then he thought of what they would have to say about GG's appointment when they got back.

He picked his drink back up. Sipped as he walked all the way to the mailbox under shade from oak trees lining the road. It seemed like the birds called out in encouragement.

A flyer for Lester's Pizza. A couple of credit card offers. A Provisions catalog. The same garbage as usual, until he got to the package on the bottom. The size of a thick notebook. Plain cardboard. Ridged, but with a soft give. Addressed to *Frank Wendall*.

A shiver passed through him. Made a few drops of tequila splatter out to stain Lester's grinning cartoon face.

He closed the mailbox door. Took the mail to the front porch. Kept the package and tucked the rest under their mat.

He made it to the barn with tequila to spare, but as soon as he dropped the package on the bench, he tipped his glass back. Set the glass aside. Reached for the bottle. Stopped himself with a shake of his head.

His fingers shook as he grabbed the package instead.

Loneliness settled across his shoulders. Frank was his own prisoner out here. Refusing to be part of a family that Gen had practically begged him to join.

He thought of how everybody who had ever been associated with him had eventually suffered. From his murdered daughter all the way to Stan getting chewed on by a gator.

Frank surprised himself by laughing. Not at his cousin's misfortune, but at the actual circumstances of his injury. How many people would believe him when he told the story of Stan getting attacked by a reptilian monster in a garage next to a marsh full of poisonous algae?

He wiped tears from his eyes before reaching into the padded envelope.

It was easier to be alone. And how easy would his life have been if he had been alone the whole time?

A shiny black plastic bag was inside. One of those anti-static bags where Stan liked to store his electronics. Frank had joked about making a hat made from the same material. How it might help keep the government from tracking him.

Stan had seemed serious about the implications, and Frank never made that joke again.

Inside the plastic bag was a new smartphone. Snapped into a thick impact-resistant case, with two separate bags. One almost the size of the phone, the other about an inch square.

He turned the phone over to find a piece of blue painter's tape stuck to the screen. *Charge me*.

He dutifully took the phone to his charger. A contactless job Mo had given him after he had lost a fourth cable.

He laid the phone on it, but got nothing. Maybe it wasn't the kind of phone that could charge like that.

Frank unplugged the charging cable from the contact-less base. Relief eased his tension when he discovered it fit into the phone's port, but still nothing. He plugged the charging base back in. Went back to the bench.

This time he poured another drink. Felt the buzzing unsteadiness all the alcohol was causing. Pleasant.

The second bag had a battery in it. Another piece of tape. *Install me.*

He sighed in frustration. Spent most of his drink figuring out how to get the phone out of its case. Then he had to put on his reading glasses to get the model number from the back of the phone so he could do an internet search on how to install the battery.

Frank felt like it was getting late, but the sun was still blazing, so he bent back over his task. Returned the phone to its case before moving to the smallest bag.

Inside was an unmarked SIM card. A little flag of tape hanging from it. *Insert me.*

The urge to throw the whole pile out the door was nearly overwhelming. But Frank patiently repeated the previous steps of removing the case, then did another search on how to insert the SIM card.

He put it all back together, but before setting it on the base, Frank poured what he knew would be his final drink of the day, despite the abundance of daylight.

The screen remained black. He hissed a silent curse, then it lit up with a swirling animation. Followed by a buzz and an electronic chime.

A white lightning bolt filled the screen, and the charger base pulsed with blue light like a digital heartbeat.

Frank looked back at the bench. There was still something in the envelope.

He swayed. Wiped sweat from his forehead. Took an unsteady step toward it before flapping his hand in dismissal. Veered toward the van to stretch out on the new carpet. Curled his fingers into the fibers. Drew a deep breath of the new smell. Hoped he only imagined the tang of blood underneath.

Chapter Nine

FRANK'S NAP was ruined by a frenzy of images. Not quite dreams. Just a broken succession of memories and feelings.

Somebody standing over him. The impression of disapproval.

Panic and fear.

Faces emerging from the darkness. Many familiar. Some of them strangers. All worried and twisted in pain.

Frank woke to the music of crickets. Tree frogs calling for mates in the failing light.

He sat up with a groan. Smacked his lips to work enough moisture into his mouth for a healthy swallow. The sun sent glowing scarlet streaks across the ground.

He made it up to his loft before peeing his pants. Emptied his bladder. Got a bottle of cold water from the fridge to fill his belly. The aspirin GG said would lower his blood pressure.

He wasn't ready to think about GG. Any more than he was ready to go in and see how his appointment had gone. He throttled those thoughts as he descended the steps back into the barn.

He snapped the lights on with a wince. Shielded his eyes as he crossed to the bench.

He avoided the phone and the envelope, lowering his head and focusing on the project he started hours ago instead.

The rear seat still needed to be stripped and recovered. His stomach growled, but the thought of food made him grimace. Just the water for now.

A buzzing distracted him. Like a distant vibration. He looked around. Rubbed his right eye to clear it. He wasn't sure what he'd expected to see. There was nothing there.

By the time Frank finished with the rear seat, the buzzing had come another three times. He grew increasingly annoyed. Unable to find its source, Frank kept looking over his shoulder as he carried the seats back to the van. First the rear seat. He tested the folding mechanism. Almost climbed in to try out the feel of the new fabric when he heard the buzzing again.

He jumped out with a growl. Stomped to the bench. Flipped the open package over. Swiped his pile of tools aside.

Then Frank saw the fading light form the corner of his eye, and realization dawned to make him feel like a frustrated idiot.

It was the new phone. Freshly charged and seeking attention.

He rushed over and snatched it up, only to sign a hiss through his teeth when he couldn't focus on the screen. Back to the bench for his reading glasses.

He saw the same repeated message. *Text HI to this number*.

Was it part of the phone's activation?

Frank rolled his eyes. Followed the prompt. The text

was away and he dropped his phone beside the package. Decided it was a good time for another break.

An irrational anger brewed as he climbed the stairs. Slapping light switches. Banging around to heat up a bowl of chicken, rice, and scrambled eggs. Floating it all in his belly with a half gallon of cold water.

He wouldn't sleep well with all that food in his system, but the water would make him have to get up and pee three or four times, so big deal.

He thought about emptying a row of Oreos, but settled for a single cookie instead. Left the lights on in the loft. Stomped back down the stairs. His knees burned with every step.

Straight to the envelope to empty the contents on the bench. Another thick envelope. Plain white paper. A stack of documents inside. Birth certificate. Driver's license. The van's registration in his new name.

The picture on the license was current. An image of how he looked now. Thin hair combed over his sunburned scalp. Short goatee. Tropical shirt. It was like he had posed for the photo, but Frank couldn't remember doing so.

Had he been drunk?

He shook his head. He couldn't have been *that* drunk.

Then Frank remembered he had just passed out in the back of the van.

It wasn't completely outside the realm of possibility that he had taken the picture himself, or had it taken by someone else … but who made the fake papers for him?

He looked at the name on the license. Just like the outside of the package. *Frank Wendall.*

The age listed him as ten years older than he actually was. He smiled at how many people were hopefully going to comment on how good he looked for his age.

The phone buzzed again.

Frank sighed as he placed the license next to the other papers. He'd been driving on a bad fake for a while now. Never drunk behind the wheel, at least.

He picked up the phone. Remembered to grab his glasses before looking at the screen. He'd have to figure out how to change the font size so he could see messages without digging for his readers every time.

He swiped the notification down.

It's about time bitch.

A door opened inside him. One he hadn't even known he'd tried to board over. Behind that door was fear. Regret. A sickening worry.

He'd heard nothing from Stan since getting here. By the time Frank had awakened in the spare bedroom, Stan was long gone. Off to have his leg treated by somebody more qualified than a powerlifting nurse and a retired Army strongman.

Not a word since.

Part of the reason Frank had drifted away from his friendships. Why he had curled in on himself. Drinking so much. Being a generally grumpy bastard.

Frank put the phone back on the bench. Closed his eyes as the tears flowed down his cheeks. As his chest tightened with equal parts pain and relief.

He wiped his nose on the back of his hand. Heaved one of the middle seats up in a bear hug and carried it out to the van. Cried into the new fabric as he scooted over on his knees to place the seat on the pedestal.

His body took him back to the bench for the second seat. Sobbing harder as he carried it to its spot in the van. His lower back tightened into a near-spasm as Frank leaned in to rock the seat onto its base.

Pushed back to slam each side door. Stumbled to the rear to slam those doors as well.

Stan was alive. Thank God.

He wondered if Mo and Gen had known the whole time. Felt resentment boil in his gut as he left the phone on the bench to go back upstairs.

Knowing Stan was okay made him lonelier than ever. Instead of being denied his cousin because of death — something he had no control over — Frank knew that he couldn't see his cousin because doing so wouldn't be fair.

Stan had suffered so much already. He had done enough for Frank, and thinking back on the package, he was *still* trying to help.

Frank couldn't allow it.

He spun back around. Held each button one at a time until he found the one that shut it off. The screen let him know that the phone was now powering down.

Stan was alive. So Frank no longer had to worry. That his cousin could live on after Frank was gone. An inevitable event that would be happening soon.

Yes, he would use the I.D. Stan had sent. The rest of the money Carmen had left when she died. Frank reached the top of the stairs again. Paused one more time.

With a sigh, he went back down for the final time. Put his new phone back on the charger.

No need to close *every* option. No reason to let the battery die.

His thighs were burning when he reached his liquor cabinet.

Nothing another bottle of tequila couldn't soothe.

Chapter Ten

IN SPITE of a massive hangover that woke Frank an hour before dawn, he still managed to be behind the wheel and on the highway before anybody in the house could wake up and come out to make small talk.

Or tell him about GG.

He had no schedule. Had plenty of time before he had to put his plan into motion — once he was able to *form* a plan — but Frank also had a nearly new interior in his van, lots of folding money, a cooler full of sandwiches, and a shiny new I.D. He wanted to avoid any complications at the house. GG's condition. Mo's judgement. The offers of sympathy from the pity circle.

He didn't listen to the radio. No podcast — even though he had gotten a LiveLyfe notification on his old phone that a new one had dropped. Ty Kirby recorded once a week, but released two shows. Frank was sure Kirby complained about *so much* work. The sound of the wind rushing into the open window was better than that man's voice anyway.

Three bottles of water before there was even a *hint* that

he would need to stop to pee. GG had often told Frank that his tendons were in danger from being so dehydrated all the time. But he never told him to quit. Never scolded him or tried to make him feel bad.

He just pointed out how suboptimal his behavior was.

Frank stopped at a Hill of Beans for a bathroom break, and a tall black coffee with room for cream. He added *brandy* to that space instead. Back on the road where he made excellent time to Rosa Alta. Nothing to do until Friday, but it beat sitting around at home and avoiding the people who still seemed to love him for sport.

Maybe they were misguided. Or mistaken. Maybe just hopeless romantics.

He hopped from happy hour to happy hour. Found dollar drafts at a bar overlooking the beach. The place was called Big League, but there wasn't a single sports reference anywhere inside.

Two tacos for two bucks at Los Compañeros.

A margarita pitcher for twelve at Sand Castle Mike's.

He pulled the shades and slept in the Walmart parking lot. Walked the beach all day. Swam and ate. Drank until the daylight was waning. Rested up, but he still couldn't relax.

He would glance at the new phone. Reach to power it up. Snatch his hand back.

He took showers at a Bernard's Truck Stop. Walked past clueless travelers mingling with drug dealers and prostitutes. A constant supply of customers from the interstate.

A grubby dump, but twelve dollars a month with his senior discount.

He pulled his gun on a pale kid who jumped off his skateboard to peer inside the van windows. All shocked eyes and hanging jaw before he split. Kicking his foot as high as it would go.

By Thursday, Frank was about to explode with nervous boredom. He took the van to a car wash. Remembered how he and Stan got into this mess when they used a white van to pick up Malick Briar.

Transported him to the nature reserve behind Stan's gym where Frank shot the fat rapist in the face. He smiled at that part of the memory. Shook his head at the reality of never being that happy again.

Though there was hope if he could get to Owens.

He gave the outside of the van a good cleaning. Vacuumed the entire interior, even though it was too new to need it. When he opened the overhead doors, the breeze blew the mist hanging in the air into his face. He closed his eyes and breathed it in.

He drove away, but it wasn't long before the heat from outside displaced the cool mist on his skin and made him roll the windows up and kick on the AC. Quiet and frosty like he knew it would be. It had cost a thousand dollars to fix the leaks in the lines and get it recharged.

That night, Frank was too wired for sleep. He needed to rest. Didn't want to rely on alcohol. But the small rechargeable fan he used didn't seem to be cutting the heat. A thousand thoughts raced through his mind, and he couldn't keep his eyes closed.

He sat up and reached for the phone. Shook his head. Flopped down with a huff of anger. Closed his eyes and told himself it was useless. He would never fall asleep.

Then he woke up with sun stabbing through the space between the side of the curtain and the edge of the window.

He sat up with a stretch. Relieved that he had passed so much time. Then collapsed in fresh frustration. There was still an entire day left.

One more day of avoiding his past. Waiting for the

future. The first *real* step he was taking since Carmen had died.

Every time he saw a twirl of red hair. The bouncy step of a woman expressing glee. The flash of a pale navel. He thought of Carmen, and an ache formed under his ribs. Then he felt guilt rise as Sarah's memory filled his mind. Then the pain became crushing emotional friction. Sticking to his efforts to get past it.

Until Jenny's sweet face would form in his mind, and he would force that door closed again. But since getting Stan's text, the doors were getting harder to keep shut.

He didn't deserve to have a woman in his life anyway. He'd had his chance … twice now. The second ended in tragedy much like the first, but he couldn't deny how full it had been before then. Like a flare that fills the sky for a moment before burning out as it falls back to earth. Not like the steady burn of his marriage.

He rolled his eyes as he wiped the soft trail of tears from his cheeks. He wouldn't have to deal with this soon enough. Always beating himself up. Feeling sorry for himself, then being angry at his own trough of self-pity.

Frank shook his head with a laugh. Doing it again. Instead of getting ready for the biggest project of his life.

He treated himself to a heavy breakfast of chocolate chip pancakes and bacon. Covered the whole mess in warm maple syrup. Smiled in shocked appreciation when the older waitress trailed her fingers across his knuckles when leaving his bill.

"I'm here through lunch if you want to come back by for the special."

Her name tag was white with a red *Sammy* written across it. Her hair was a washed-out blonde that showed a creeping of gray from the roots.

She had experience in her face and body that Frank

found delightful. Lines and curves that told a story he wouldn't mind hearing more than once. But he couldn't be distracted, no matter that he didn't deserve her attention.

"I just might." He paid with cash and gave her a wave on his way out. It was easy for Frank to tell himself that he might check Sammy out after this was all over, since he doubted his survival, and not even all that deep down.

But there was a pep in his step as Frank walked back to the van.

The good mood persisted through most of the day. Even when he skipped the lunch special for a meatball panini from a Round The World food truck. A side of hushpuppies to go with the theme. Sitting on the beach under a cool cloudy sky with a coconut slushie he'd bolstered with two shots of rum.

The closer it came to dark, the more Frank felt like he was speeding. From the top of the hill to where the bottom disappeared in roiling mist. How much speed would he gain? What awaited him at the bottom?

He ended up pulling into his usual spot next to the dumpster. Listened to Kirby's new show. Watched cars arrive, trying to identify any one of them as the men he was waiting for, only sure of the gray Ford Escape that the cop had gotten out of last week as Kirby was finishing his smoke break.

Frank didn't need to hear their discussion to understand it. Both had flushed faces of anticipation. Three more men joined them, and Frank studied *their* expressions. None of them were leading girls inside. No mysterious bags held between them like Carmen and Preston. Maybe they were just getting ready for some Texas Hold 'Em.

They all filed inside after Kirby. Frank imagined the sound of the door slamming behind them. Like a gunshot.

He started the van. Backed it out into the street.

Turned left at the corner where the small picnic tables sat at the side of Kirby's studio, then into an alley so he could pull back onto the one-way street running parallel with the row of buildings under the upper floor. Under a tree that dripped sap on anything that parked there. Next to a dog park where Frank had never seen a single dog.

Now, if he had to leave in a hurry, he had a nearly straight shot to Dalton Avenue, then less than a mile to the highway. He wouldn't need to rush off, though. He grabbed his multi-tool, the lockpick, and a tiny bottle of 3-in-1 oil. He was just going to look, but he still reached behind his back to make sure the pistol was in its holster when he got out.

Chapter Eleven

FRANK WALKED with his assumed confidence. Just out for the evening to get some air.

The breeze was dying down, and the still air clung to him. Sweat made his entire back feel greasy and slick. He kept his eyes fixed on the corner of the patio. Prepared an excuse as he dropped down to feel for the recorder under Kirby's table.

He would tell anybody that caught him that he was looking for a discarded cigarette butt. Kirby could vouch for him — or at least testify that he had seen him bumming for a cigarette a week ago. He'd be unlikely to forget their verbal exchange.

It seemed to take forever to get the screwdriver head lined up with the first screw, but it slid right into the second screw with ease. He rubbed over the ground with his off hand before grabbing the edge of the table for support. He was up with the recorder in his pocket, and a decent butt hanging between his fingers. He hoped he wouldn't have to light it up.

He headed into the alley. Hugging the rear wall to stay

in the shadows. The music from the shops and restaurants sounded distant and muffled. The traffic sounded like ocean waves. Or he was hearing the *actual* ocean. He smiled to himself as he turned into the alcove at the bottom of the fire escape.

It was just as unsteady as he remembered, and he gave a silent prayer of thanks upon reaching the top. He leaned into the door. Rested his fingers on the handle and closed his eyes. When he pushed on the handle, it rotated with a grinding squeak. He winced at the noise, then sighed with relief. It was noisy, but it was still unlocked.

He released the handle. Pulled out the little oil bottle. Dribbled a few drops on each hinge. All down the gap between the edge of the door and the frame. A good squirt into where the latch engaged the strike plate. Another one around where the handle went into the circular trim plate. Put the bottle back and waited a slow count of twenty before trying again.

This time the handle turned without a sound. He gritted his teeth and gave a gentle pull. The door opened with a low groan of rusty metal. No alarm. No shouts or flashing lights. Barely enough room for him to stand out of the way of the swinging door. He squeezed past. Pulled the door shut behind him, and paused to let his eyes adjust to the dark.

He was in the alcove at the end of the hallway he had seen in the blueprints. He squinted around, and just like he had thought, there was nothing there but debris piled in one corner, a fire extinguisher sitting on the floor, and a push broom with a broken handle. Nobody had been down here in who knew how long. Maybe years.

The sound of laughter made him freeze. From the other end of the hall. Male voices. The clink of glass bottles in a toast.

Frank worked himself to the corner. Listening to how the floor responded to his weight. He didn't hear any cracks or pops, but the sound of the music in the shop below them filtered up. More of a vibration. He doubted that anybody down there could hear the laughter. They probably wouldn't even hear any screams.

He pressed his nose to the wall. Turned enough to just look at the corner. The big room at the top of the stairs — the open area that was supposed to be shared reception — was blazing with light. Flickering patterns on the floor confused him until he realized it was the reflection of a TV. Men doing *men* things. Probably watching whatever sport was currently in season. Frank had never really cared about sports, but he understood its appeal.

The tribalism. The fan ownership. It was the same as rooting for the good guy in a movie. Only your guy was *always* the good guy.

The five doorways were on the left. Each one dark. The windows on the front wall to his right were covered in heavy fabric. Like padded quilts.

More laughter made him draw back into the dark. He wished he had planted the recorder up here. But then he would miss what was on the one from the picnic table. He couldn't have done both. He only had the one recorder, and getting another one would require interacting with Mo again. He wasn't ready just yet.

He couldn't hear the words the men were saying, but he could catch a lot of the tone. The *mood*. It was childlike excitement. An almost giddy energy. He had been to his fair share of poker games. Hung around with plenty of men doing traditionally male activities. He remembered the feeling of release from some of them. From being let out of the house alone.

Like boys without their parents around.

What he was feeling from the end of the hall was different. It was men on the cusp of behaving with abandon. The kind of feeling he imagined was in the room where the bank robbers planned their heist ... if they were all twelve years old.

He couldn't risk going into the hallway. Not for a drunken card game. On paper, this was the most innocent activity to find inside a dusty old building. A bunch of guys hiding from their wives and bosses. Just getting up to some shenanigans. And *that's* not what worried Frank. It wasn't what they were doing. It was what they were planning.

He backed toward the door. Pulled his hand back around when he realized he had been holding the pistol's grip. Opened the door to a night much louder than he remembered, but after the relative quiet of the upper floor, he wasn't surprised. After swinging around the edge of the door and closing it behind him, he leaned back with a sigh. If they hadn't heard him open it and come in, they definitely hadn't heard him leave.

He made it to the alley without the fire escape collapsing into a mangled heap. Crossed to the fence and walked back to the van without looking at the buildings behind him.

When he climbed into the driver's seat, the anxiety hit like a seizure. His teeth chattered as he curled forward with a shivering convulsion. Like he had been overtaken by a freezing wind. His abs tightened into cramps, and his toes curled, making the flip-flops creak.

Stupid to still be wearing them. To be going up there with no plan. Just one man by himself with no backup and no way to defend himself against so many at once. And no *legal* defense either.

What a foolish old man he was.

He reached a shaking hand out to close the door.

Hugged himself and pushed back into his seat. Deep breaths as pain in his neck swelled. Burning and radiating. He wanted to pound his chest. Tell his heart to stop being so dramatic.

He leaned forward to rest his head on the wheel. Got the key in the ignition without looking. Started the engine. The comfort of the rumble made his shoulders relax. The deep vibration that hit through the floor to roll up through his bones. For the first time, he began to doubt his ability to see it through. Not just the nagging question of whether or not he had it in him to get it done. But a real concern that he just wouldn't make it.

His eyes snapped open, and he sat up in alarm. Like he had fallen asleep, only for some strange sound to wake him from a bad dream, but there was nothing there. His heart was steady. No pain in his neck or chest. He reached up and wiped oily sweat from his forehead. He looked around, and everything was as it had been when he had climbed behind the wheel.

It could only have been a few minutes at most. And that was concerning enough.

He decided to wait until he was home to listen to the recording. Or better yet, get home and have a few drinks. Then some sleep. *Then* listen to the recording.

Chapter Twelve

THE SOUND of the lawnmower woke him up. Like it was sitting under his window. Even if he blocked out the morning sun, rolled over and hugged his pillow, the noise would keep him awake.

Either Mo was trying to wake him up on purpose, or there was a patch of grass in desperate need of trimming right outside. Some mutant strain that grew while you looked at it. Unlike the *rest* of the grass in the yard that Mo insisted on cutting. Short, brown, and brittle.

Frank kicked his sheet off. Put his foot down on an empty beer can. Kicked it aside so he could stand. Stumbled over to the coffee. When he dug into the little tray of pods, all he found was pumpkin spice. Something he had probably gotten from Gen. He shrugged. Jammed it into the machine and hit the button.

Then he hissed in surprise and darted over to get a cup out of the cabinet. Had it under the dispenser just before the coffee started sputtering out of the nozzle. A few steaming drops splattered onto his skin, and he jerked his hand up to flap it through the air as he danced back.

With his stinging finger in his mouth, he walked to the balcony door. Stepped out into the light and leaned over the side railing. There was Mo. Sitting on the idling lawnmower. Arms crossed as he waited, staring up at Frank's window.

Frank waved. Got no response. Leaned out farther to wave *both* arms. Mo glanced over. Then he put his hands over his heart in an *oh, I didn't see you there* pantomime. He dropped his big feet to the pedals, put the mower in gear, and waved goodbye with an enthusiastic grin.

The mower rattled and bounced all the way back to the shed by the RV. Frank watched until Mo disappeared around the front corner of the house. He shook his head as he turned back inside to get his coffee. He had needed to get up anyway.

The flavor of the coffee made him shudder in disgust, but at least it was hot. The pile of beer cans on the floor — coupled with his headache — told him he didn't need to be drinking any alcohol for a while, but when he sat at the kitchen table, he reached for the brandy. Just to spice up that pumpkin.

It barely made it tolerable. One notch above *I can't even.*

He scrubbed the grit from his eyes as he settled in. Pulled his journal close, but hesitated to open the laptop. Stan had always told him that technology was his friend. Even though Frank wasn't quite yet convinced, it wasn't the technology that made him pause.

He took another sip. Blew out another sigh. Opened the laptop and plugged the recorder into it. Readied himself to play the file. Hit the button and sat back with a sneer of dread.

It only recorded when the sound around it was above a certain decibel threshold. A lot of wind noise. Car stereos.

A loud exhaust or two. And voices. The first of which Frank recognized right away.

Ty Kirby speaking to somebody, but there were no responses. Frank assumed he was on the phone. Then Kirby called the person *babe*. Must be talking to a girl-friend. *Whining* to her was more like it. Something about how it was the night of the big game, and he would make it up to her.

The poker game Frank had seen?

Then Frank heard the first name. "Hines said it would be the last one for a while," Kirby squeaked. "I promise I'll make it up to you, babe. Week after next, yes. I *swear*."

Hines. Frank paused the recording to put it in his journal.

A few minutes into listening again, and he was convinced Kirby's girlfriend was a saint. Constantly listening to her boyfriend — the glory hound — complaining about how he wasn't appreciated. Maybe it was his wealth. Sometimes love didn't start out blind, but was blinded by money.

When the wind noise followed by digital silence told him this particular conversation was done, Frank clipped it out and put it in a folder he titled, Kirby Kisses Babe's Booty.

He wasn't entirely sure he had done it right until the next part of the recording started playing.

When he was finished with the entire week, he had a folder for every conversation, but eight of them were just Kirby talking to Babe. He consolidated them all into that original folder. Surveyed the names of all the other ones.

Whenever there had been a person mentioned, Frank had noted it in his journal. Names of any people talking to Kirby on the recording got a star next to them. Names of men that seemed to recur in reference to Friday night activities got their own page. There were six of them.

Jacobs, Hines, Rosedale, Hernandez, Wilson, and Reed.

They each got their own folder with copies of conversations that featured them. The only other names that got folders were Owens — mentioned quite often, and Frank — mentioned only a disappointingly few times.

The final folder was a miscellaneous place to catch the odd noises and snatches of distant voices. Conversations with no relevance. He copied them all to two different flash drives. One that he would store in his loft. The other would go in the van. Once he copied his notes over to both, there would be a nice pool of evidence against Kirby and his *friends*.

Stan would be so proud of him.

Frank was too sickened by what he had heard to eat, so he pulled a few beers out instead. Calories *and* alcohol. By the time he was done with his image search, he could have a good buzz going to face it all again. A little something to numb the pain and anger.

He sat back down with a bottle and an opener and a plan. Couple each name with a search term. Rose County Sheriff's Office. Willett County. Enola PD. Rosa Alta PD. Anything else that might get him an official image of the men meeting at the Watchtower. An image he could study so he knew who he was killing.

Most of them, like Lieutenant Carl Wilson from the Enola Police Department, were easy hits. But they were all in the habit of only using each other's last names, so without a first name, a few of them were difficult. They required multiple searches, but the most difficult had been Justin Hines.

He was the first cop Frank had seen talking to Kirby,

and it was only luck that led to his identification. He was in a picture standing next to Wilson at a funeral, identified by the caption. He was an investigator in the Florida Attorney General's office.

That put Ty Kirby closer to the top than Frank had thought. And it put Frank in more danger. Even as close as Frank was to being done, it didn't matter. In spite of all the public scrutiny into the Tallahassee incident — peddled by Kirby himself — and the *official* wariness in supporting the previous members, the men had wasted no time in setting up a new den.

And it would happen again and again. Proven by the conversations Frank had recorded where they detailed what they had done. At first, just trickles here and there. Girlfriends. Prostitutes. Any woman foolish enough to agree to go there.

Frank imagined the desperate shock of those women after walking into what they had been told was an empty room only to find eager men waiting.

Frank's heart ached at every soul who had been humiliated inside that place. All the abuse. But he couldn't go in and start swinging a bat. The men had a defense. All the women had been of legal consenting age, and the bondage *fun* had been consensual, they would say.

But Hines had spoken to Kirby about the *girls* they were bringing in two weeks. One Friday after the game. Had he just been using a word? Or were they *really* girls?

Frank had heard many terms for the women being brought to the upper floor. Chicks. Bitches. Skanks. Women. Kirby had even called his own girlfriend a cunt and a cum dumpster. Hines had laughed. Then what sounded like a slap to Kirby's shoulder.

This was the first time Frank had heard the word *girls*. Or perhaps he had heard it before — occasionally — but without the emphasis Hines seemed to use. The *weight* Frank now heard in the word.

He had told Ty there would be a *couple* of girls. Just two? Shared between six men?

His stomach roiled with suppressed rage.

It didn't matter that Owens was temporarily out of the game. It just left Kirby and Hines as the point men. Besides, if Owens could hear the thing Frank had heard in the recording, he might not be nearly as trusting when it came to his prior allies.

It seemed that the protection Owens thought he had inside the force was waning. Except for a strong foothold in upper management protecting him, the cop wasn't nearly as untouchable as he used to be. Frank took pride in knowing *he* was partly responsible for the shift in attitude.

Owens had been able to hide his own agenda, shielded from the cops he was playing by officers higher up in the food chain. But a once-essential cog was apparently becoming an embarrassment. Frank now knew he didn't have to look for Owens himself.

Other cops like Hines would do it for him. As long as Frank raised a big enough stink.

According to Hines and Kirby, there had already been a few meetings in the upper floor next to the Watchtower for some initial "fun." Some adult BDSM. Trains and gang bangs. All on young *adult* women whose consent was questionable at best.

Hines had made it clear that there was an interest in *younger* participants. Spoken of as casually as discussing a weekly poker game.

Kirby had expressed his extreme regret in the fact that he couldn't make it to the next "session." He'd said it was a *family* thing, but Frank had heard the conversation between Kirby and Babe where he had apologized for forgetting their anniversary. Promised to make it up to her next Friday. A fancy dinner at Thompson's Steakhouse.

Frank had taken Sarah several years ago. Neither of them had been impressed. Maybe the place had improved since then. But probably not.

So six names: the men that were supposedly meeting at Kirby's studio — sans Kirby — to have their *fun* on the upper floor. These six men were going to have the experience of their lives, but Frank doubted it would end up being anywhere near the calliope of pitch-black delight they were planning.

Chapter Thirteen

FRANK COULDN'T STAY in the barn while he waited. There was too much potential to be confronted by things he just wasn't yet ready to face. Or just *one* thing. GG. Frank burned at the thought, but he knew if he died in the Watchtower, he wouldn't have to watch GG fade away. Wouldn't have to keep seeing the disappointment when he told him no.

He couldn't sit on the beach at Rosa Alta either. With a bottle in his hand while he looked up at the windows. Ready to charge in and save a girl — even if it meant ruining the plan. But maybe he could end up there after a nice drive.

He packed a bag and a cooler, and he fled. He ran away. Something Sarah had often accused him of. Even with the little things. Since before Jenny was born.

He always gave in.

Jenny had been a small bundle of energy. A hard charger from the moment she learned how to walk. He had adored her. Struggled with giving her everything she asked for while trying to teach her discipline and respect.

He thought he had believed in spanking. Little corrective swats. But the first time he had pulled her off her feet to smack her little behind, he had cried more than her.

"I'm sowwy, Dada!"

For days he had been terrified that she would no longer love him. He hated how it had made him feel like a bully. How he towered over her. Descended upon her in anger. Made her feel helpless.

He had never spanked her again. Love and gentle communication. Firm rules. He and Sarah standing united. And they had raised a good person. He often dreamed about what she would have been like as an adult.

Calm and wise and beautiful.

She had been six years old when they first sorted through her growing mountain of toys. Where some children had a box, Jenny had a *whole* room. When she got older, they converted it into an art studio. Mostly messy painting, clay sculptures that all looked alike, and Legos. But before that it had been wall-to-wall dolls.

And she had known which tiny boots went to which tiny outfit went to which tiny doll.

Every day for a week, he and Sarah had taken the older toys — broken, forgotten, or just less used — and they had put them in a plastic bag by the door. Neither had said a word about it, but of course they did it while Jenny was asleep. Finally, when they had two bags full, they took them to Goodwill.

He couldn't even leave the parking lot without breaking down in tears. Sarah had looked at him in confusion. Like somebody had asked her to help them remove their spleen. "Frank ... what is it, honey?"

He jabbed a finger at the thrift shop in angry accusation. "We're throwing away her childhood!"

They had gotten through it. Just as they had gotten

through everything. The fear that Jenny would end up deaf from her persistent ear infections. Her fall from the top of the refrigerator because that was where Frank had hidden the oatmeal cream pies. Losing her for a heart-wrenching moment at the county fair.

Sarah's ovarian cysts. His recovery after getting shot. When she begged for him to retire. Or to get a job in security at Jenny's school. Arguments about Stan. About work. About how unfulfilled she felt. Putting her life on hold for an older man. Then again for her baby girl.

She often asked when it was going to be *her* turn, and he would often look at Jenny and wonder what else Sarah could possibly need.

As he pulled onto the highway to head toward Heirloom Cove, he wondered how he had never seen it before. The signs of her unhappiness. The mental illness under the surface that was ready to burst through given the right catalyst. Like a murdered daughter. A cheating husband.

A life that hadn't turned out the way she had wanted it to.

But he had ignored his *own* problems for so long, it was no wonder he was blind to other people's. It was hard to see what you were unwilling to look at.

There had been a time when they loved each other. Deeply, and with breathtaking passion. A life he had never dared to dream of. But good things never lasted forever ... all things came to an end ... Murphy's law ... blah blah blah.

He passed the hours in silence. Pretending Sarah was next to him. Jenny playing quietly in the back. By the time he got to the cemetery, it was early afternoon. A scorching sun but a cool breeze.

He didn't dare go to their graves. Even as different as he looked, he couldn't risk being seen. He couldn't imagine somebody actually watching the graves of his dead wife and daughter, but he could imagine what it would be like if they were. So he stopped at the first grave off of the path leading away from the parking lot.

Meagan Arnette. Born in 1974. Died in 1990. Not yet a woman.

Frank took his hat off. Shuffled his feet on the perfect grass. "Hi Meagan. You don't know me, but my name is Frank." He tipped his head toward the slope that led away. Down toward the edge of the lake where his family plot was. "I'm sure you know Jenny and Sarah, right? You all talk to each other around here, right?"

This was silly.

He growled a sigh through his nose. Forced a smile. Looked back at the small stone at his feet. "I can't be seen talking to them. Bad men might be watching. I'm also not sure they would even *want* me over there. I've messed up some things pretty bad, Meagan."

He shook his head with a bitter laugh. "It's not fair for me to ask you, but could you tell them? That I'm sorry. That I'm doing the best I can. That I'm okay, and that I love them. Could you tell them that?"

Several minutes passed as he crumpled his hat in one hand and then the other. While he looked up at the sky like the words he needed would be written in clouds. He argued with himself about even being here, let alone staying. But he could smell the water. Hear the birds. See the colors of the flowers planted and placed at gravesites.

"There's not much left to say. Nothing worth apologizing for anymore. I just want them to know that it's coming to the end now. The finish line, as they say. Good or bad, it will be finished, and I can finally focus on something else. Maybe accept the help that Rogers offered.

Maybe help somebody *else*. The sky's the limit. That's another thing they say."

He suddenly felt foolish. Talking to a dead relative through a third party that was also dead. He threw his hands out in frustration. "I'm sorry." He looked down at her name. "I'm sorry you died so young, Meagan. Just tell them I was here, okay?"

He hurried back to the van like he was being followed. Climbed inside and slammed the door. He glanced up at himself in the rearview mirror. Curled his lip in disgust.

He started the van and drove down to the water. Looked out over the glittering reflections. He turned toward the nearest exit. Managed to leave without screeching his tires, but he had a long drive ahead of him. He wanted the cemetery behind him. No need to linger.

He was coming back soon.

Chapter Fourteen

THE ENOLA PUBLIC Library was closed by the time he got into town, but that was okay. There was a Staples out in a shopping center under a giant water tower painted to look like a jellyfish. *ENOLA* was written across it to look like jolts of electricity. Frank had driven past it every time he had come into Rosa Alta, and not once had he been curious enough to ask about it.

He just didn't care about the history of a town he wouldn't be in much longer.

Inside the painful bright of artificial store lighting, Frank paid the thirty-five cents per page to make a copy of his journal. Even the fitness portion. All of his notes about Jenny's death, all the way up to his discoveries at Ty Kirby's studio. Bought a mailer box on his way out and got back in the van to head to a late dinner. A burger bar across the highway called Brisket Doug's.

Warm lights over the tables. Soft jazz. Righteous hamburgers, and hundreds of craft beers on tap. Stan would love it, and that seemed appropriate. Many of their best times, and most of their best conversations, had been had over food.

Not just he and Stan, but he and Sarah too. Like how they planned to try to have a baby over the first time she made that chicken marsala that used to drive him crazy. Meeting for lunch while he was working weekends after his promotion. The ritual of taking Jenny out for ice cream. Making macadamia nut and white chocolate chip cookies for the bake sale every year.

Food used to be a huge part of his life, but lately it had *become* his life. Actually, it was more like alcohol had become his life, but why pick at nits?

He ordered a stout and a plate of loaded nachos to start while he assembled his copies. Slid them into the mailer, along with the flash drive with the copy of the recordings. He addressed the mailer to the Stit AC company out of Galveston, Texas. Stan's dummy company that owned the whole beach at Playa Dolor.

He paused when his server came back with the appetizer. Ordered the Big Brisket Basket, and took his time with the nachos while he waited. He wanted to write a letter, but he didn't know what to say. *This is my last will and testament? To whom it may concern? If you're reading this, then I'm dead?*

At least a note, though. Stan would be able to figure out what all of it meant, but he should write *something*. He slid a scrap of paper over. Doodled a smiley face in the upper left corner. Then he wrote his note. *Don't be a bitch like me. Finish the job.* He put the note in with the rest. Put one of Brisket Doug's menus on top. Sealed it up and pushed it aside to make room for his plastic basket full of meat.

It was a little dry, but the cornbread was fantastic, and it wasn't often he could find fried okra. The beer was the perfect companion to the smoky barbeque, and the peanut butter pie he finished with was rich and creamy. Almost *too* decadent. He left no scraps when he was done.

He drove back to Staples to drop the mailer in the big blue mailbox out front. Left town in favor of staying at the rest stop two exits down. Sat in the dark and wondered if he was doing the right thing. He drained the last beer in the cooler before getting up to head inside for a pee. Brush his teeth before turning in.

Of course he was doing the right thing. The only thing he *could* do. So the question was actually, was he doing the thing *right*?

Back in the van, and he had to admit he wasn't. There was much he could have done better. From his marriage all the way to GG wanting the pain to go away. But this close to the end, was there really any reason to keep going over the details of every single mistake? Or to relive the guilt of killing? Or the shame of relishing the opportunity to kill again?

He didn't think it was particularly productive, but it was the only way he knew how to live. It had become a habit. As destructive as Ty Kirby's tobacco abuse. He crawled into the back and fired up his little fan. Wondered why he couldn't have been a better man as he fell asleep.

DESPITE THE MORNING sunshine streaming in, everything looked dull and gray when he woke up. His bladder was so full, he had trouble standing up straight. Made it to the urinal inside just in time. Took a hobo's bath in the sink before going back to the van.

For what he had planned for the evening, his day was pretty tame. To Rosa Alta where he would do yoga on the beach to loosen up for the later activity. Keep his heartrate up, but not jacked. A big breakfast and a hearty lunch, then nothing else but water. It would be a shame to fail at the end because of a calf cramp.

Every passing moment brought him closer. An electric energy buzzing in his skull. The anticipation making it hard to concentrate on anything. Packing and repacking his backpack. Having his clothes ready. Like he was laying them out for a date. Just a sensible outfit that *wasn't* a loose tropical short and cargo shorts for once.

After a lunch of three Jersey Mike's subs he ate out under a tree next to the truck stop, he decided to get after it. It was too early, but he couldn't go home yet, so he went in for a shower. Took his time with his hair. Carefully edged his goatee. He even trimmed his eyebrows. He was vibrating with excitement when he took his toiletry bag back to the van.

His breathing exercises couldn't get it under control. Water and meditation didn't work. A protein bar didn't help. He realized the only thing that was going to ease his growing mania was the thing itself. The release of the job.

It was still too early.

He looked at the candy wrapper crumpled up in a ball on the center console of the van. The bugs smeared across the windshield. The shiny skin of his cheeks in the rearview mirror reflection. He nodded to himself. That could kill some time, and the van deserved a good cleaning. Only God knew what it was going to be stained with by the end.

Chapter Fifteen

THE TRIP to the carwash had the feeling of ritual, even though it was only the second time he had been there. He closed the overhead doors, sealing himself in the bay. Soaped and scrubbed. All the parts that didn't appear to need it. Then up under the wheel wells. Balancing on the rear bumper to get the roof.

He felt like a squire washing the knight's horse. Polishing his shield. Too bad he didn't feel like the knight.

After taking his time on the exterior, running through almost thirty dollars on soap and wax, he moved to the inside. A fresh vacuum. Windex on the inside of the glass. 303 Protectant on all the plastic and rubber. He finished by spreading a thick sheet of plastic over the carpet between the middle seats. He held it down with four magnets, each one with a hundred pounds of pull.

He felt light after opening the doors to the setting sun. Floated up into the driver's seat. A strange impulse made him pull the Van Halen cassette out of the glovebox, and he cruised the streets of Rosa Alta to the wow and flutter of "Panama." He winced whenever David Lee Roth went for a high note.

He got to Alta Drive. Rolled past his dumpsters. Turned at the patio to end up backing into his spot under the sap bomber. A shame he had just spent so much time and money washing the van. And there were *still* no dogs in the little park.

Pressure was building in his neck. Tension growing between his shoulder blades. His skin alternated between goosebumps and warm flushing.

He looked at the cars parked nearby. In his little lot and the one across the street in front of the beach. He saw Hines' Ford. Had no idea what the other men had driven. The Watchtower's patio was lit by a dim light shining through the side door's window. Nobody was outside in the alley. Just the normal noise from the shops. Shouts and music from the beach.

Frank got out to take a deep breath. He put his hands on his thighs so he could push his shoulders as high as possible. Got every single ounce of air he could. Walked to the rear doors. Wiped the sweat from his face before reaching inside for his gear. Shut the door with one hand. Slung the pack up behind him with the other.

His backpack was made of black canvas. Heavy duty with double seams. It pulled his shoulders back and down with its weight. Full of random objects that on first inspection might seem odd, but innocent.

Two five-pound plates. Rusty Olympic weights he'd bought at a thrift store. A few lengths of chain. One, three, and four feet. Elastic knee wraps — woven bands about six feet long for stabilizing the knees during heavy squats. He'd seen guys wrap them tight enough to turn their calves the color of a bad bruise before they finished their reps. Might be good for tying somebody up. Or maybe he'd have to wrap his knees for support when he had to dump a body.

The duct tape and zip-ties bent the relative innocence of the rest of the contents, but the first-aid kit and multi-tool were in every camper's tent.

The pouches on the outside were packed with protein bars. Two bottles of water, and a packet of electrolytes.

His gun was in its holster, nestled in the small of his back, but Frank didn't think he would need it. He almost left it in the van.

He didn't see any more lights as he walked down the alley to the fire escape. Before going to the carwash an hour and a half ago, Frank had watched Kirby hustle out. On his way to his promised dinner date with his girlfriend. No doubt regretting his absence on the upper floor, but like the rest of the men knew — and even Frank himself — there would be more girls later.

Frank held his backpack overhead as he descended the ladder with one hand. Kept himself from looking around suspiciously at the landing. Upstairs to the door, where he entered like an owner, easing the door to pass through with his pack held out in front of him.

Closed the door behind him. Rolled the lock over with his teeth gritted in nervous caution.

It made an oily click that he felt more than heard.

Faint sounds still drifted up from the street. Same for music from the shops below. Frank had sat in the dark at the end of this hall and listened many times, though he had never told anyone what he was doing here. Only that it was just another weekender at Rosa Alta.

Faint noise from down the hall. Excited voices. Creaking floors. Frank wondered if their activities ever caused alarm below them. He cocked his ear, but heard only a general wash of sound. He could imagine anything happening up here being dismissed down below.

Unless things got louder than usual.

More violent.

Frank set his backpack on the floor. Leaned it against the wall. Unzipped it as if avoiding a trap. Slow and easy. He slid the medium chain out one link at a time. Wrapped it around his right fist until his knuckles throbbed.

Filled his left cargo pocket with a bundle of zip-ties. The roll of duct tape. He smirked in disgust at the thought that there was probably plenty more in one of the rooms.

Took one of the weight plates in his left hand. Twisted to stand, but froze when his sneakers squeaked on the wooden floor.

Frank was used to wearing flip-flops. Not very good in a confrontation. He thought about going barefoot. Shook his head like he was arguing with a mime.

Drew a deep breath. Held it as he stood tall and peeked around the corner.

The windows were all covered in heavy construction blankets. Frank knew it was more for blocking sound and light than for protecting the glass from renovations.

The reception area at the end was ablaze with light. Nobody there. No shadows shifting to indicate movement. No TV or poker game.

More voices raised in … all Frank could really identify was *emotion*. He wasn't close enough to know if the voice was happy or sad or angry. Only that it was male.

Out of the five doors along the hall, only the last two appeared occupied. Light shining out into the hall.

The three doors nearest him seemed dark, but that didn't mean they were empty. Maybe a last-minute change brought a third girl, and her abuser wanted to stay in the dark.

Frank pressed himself into the wall as he slid around the corner. Kept his feet as close to the baseboard as he could. Moved on his toes to the nearest door. Whirled through the doorway to put his back against the wall. Hands up. Staring into the dusty dark of the empty space.

He nodded to himself. Slowed his breathing. Pulling air through his open mouth so he wouldn't make gasping noises. Sweat trickled down the sides of his neck under his jaw.

The voices were louder. Plus *another* voice. Whimpering and crying. Then the sound of a blow. The bright snap of skin contacting skin.

Frank threw himself into the hallway. Rushed along the wall to the next door. The floor groaned underfoot as he spun inside, making himself as small as he possibly could. Surveyed the dark room while pretending to be oh so invisible.

He heard another small voice in a drawn-out whine.

Then a much deeper voice muttering a curse.

Gagging and coughing. More slaps. Laughter and moans.

Frank wanted to tear off his ears. But he needed to continue, despite the terror of seeing something far worse than what his mind could imagine.

His memory flashed on the images from Jenny's crime scene — there could be nothing worse here than seeing the grisly remains of his dead daughter.

He dropped into a crouch and moved down the hall. No sound but the brush of his toes through the dust. Another pause in the darkness with the sounds of an unimaginable reality washing over him. Tears floating crystal shards of light in front of his eyes.

A girl's voice raised in pain.

A stifled sob.

The sound of a fist in flesh.

A splatter of fluid. Cruel laughter.

Frank wiped his eyes on his forearms. Tightened his grip on the plate. Raised his chained fist.

His face tingled with numbness, but Frank could feel the smile stretching his lips as he stepped into the hallway.

Chapter Sixteen

THERE WAS a loud *whoo* from next door just as he entered. Followed by a cry of pain. Frank's mind made note of the noise. Blocked it out as he took in the horror of what was in front of him.

A girl standing on her tiptoes in the center of a large sheet of black plastic. A thin rope around her neck stretched up to a block and tackle suspended by an old light fixture hanging from the cracked plaster ceiling, hands bound behind her back.

Tears poured from her bloodshot eyes. Snot bubbled over the red rubber ball strapped into her mouth.

Pale skin mottled by strips of red. Some already bruising at the edges.

Her eyes widened into shock as Frank filled the doorway. Her shivering body tightened in alarm.

Hines stood in front of her with his hand drawn back. A wooden yardstick cocked back to deliver another blow.

She was so small.

Hines was still clothed. The only concession made to

his activity was the jacket draped over the back of a wooden chair. Tie loosened. Collar unbuttoned.

A wrinkled blanket at the girl's feet was covered in various implements Hines was planning to use. Or ones he *already* had.

Frank wasn't in time to stop the swing, and Hines delivered a cracking shot that hit under her left breast. A fresh stripe over the girl's ribs. She cried out into the gag. Coughed and snorted as her shifting weight put pressure on the rope. Face deepening into scarlet. Eyes rolling back in panic.

Frank could only imagine what his own face looked like, but when Hines turned around, the shocked expression served as an excellent clue. To see a crazy drifter charging into the room must have stopped his heart in confusion.

He took a half step to the side, and Frank finished his entry by swinging a savage kick up into Hines' balls. Frank grunted out his effort as the top of his shoe made crushing contact.

The yardstick clattered to the floor, and Hines bent over the blow with a gagging wheeze of surprised pain. Frank pulled his foot back. Planted it for stability. Raised his left hand to fire the edge of the five-pound plate into the ridge of bone over his opponent's right eye.

A greasy crunch, and an arcing spray of blood as Hines' head snapped back, and Frank jumped forward to wrap him in a hug. Hold him up on unsteady legs so he could ease him to the floor.

The sound of him falling would have alerted the party next door. There were five men over there, if everyone showed. Frank hated himself for the thought, but he hoped they could be occupied with their *fun* for a few moments longer.

He set the weight on the blanket. Unwound the chain from his fist. Rolled Hines over so he wouldn't choke on the blood dribbling down his face into his mouth. Frank could see the gleam of his skull through the gaping wound.

Frank dragged Hines' arms behind his back. Pulled the zip-ties from his pocket. Ratcheted three of them on Hines' wrists. Cinching them down until they almost broke the skin.

He turned to move down to the man's ankles, but Hines bucked under him. Grunted a confused question. A pool of crimson spread under his head like a bloody aura. Frank spread himself out to put as much of his weight down as he could. Dug for the tape in his pocket.

His other hand scraped over damp cloth. He looked up to find the girl's panties snagged in his groping fingers. He could smell the urine from an arm's length away.

He raised up to plant his knees in the middle of Hines' back. Then a hop to drive his weight down. Drove the air from his lungs in a groaning rush.

Frank grabbed a handful of hair and pulled Hines' head back as hard as he could. Stuffed the saturated panties into his gaping mouth. Shifted to plant his knee under his jaw, then pulled a strip of tape from the roll.

He got the adhesive started. Pulled the roll so it wrapped around Hines' head. All the way over the start of the strip at the edge of his mouth. Around another full turn.

Then Frank stood. Pulled his foot back and drove it up between the man's legs.

Hines flopped in agony. Rolled onto his side and curled up. Retched and swallowed. Frank dropped down and hooked Hines' feet under his arm. Three more zip-ties to bind his ankles. Then he forced Hines onto his stomach.

Bent his knees and zip-tied his wrists and hands together. Like a hog ready for roasting.

Frank didn't care if Hines choked to death on blood or vomit. He just wanted him out of commission while he went into the next room.

Frank tiptoed back to the door. Put the side of his head toward the hallway. Grunting. Wet slapping. Deep moans of pleasure. Squealing moans of pain.

Rough laughter.

He closed his eyes and turned back into Hines' room. He knew the plan for these girls was murder. What would probably be a merciful end to who knew how many hours of torture and abuse.

He couldn't cry now. He needed to focus.

He jogged on light feet. Right to the black tarp where he dropped beside her. On his knees, she was only a head taller than him. She held her head tipped back. Nostrils flared to get air. She rolled her eyes down to keep him in view.

He held his hands out in front of her. His fingers spread wide. Pointed at the gag. "If I take that out, will you be quiet?"

Her jaw muscles bulged. Her eyebrows drew together.

"Please. You can't scream. Or make *any* noise. I'm so sorry, but I can't alert the men in the next room, and we don't have much time."

A fresh trail of tears streamed down her temple. She blinked them away. Nodded against the rope around her throat.

Frank shuffled around her on his knees. Saw that abuse to her skin continued around to her back. He opened the buckle at the nape of her neck. Loosed the strap over the gag.

The girl tried to spit it out, but she didn't have enough

movement in her neck to toss it aside. Frank muttered an apology before hooking it out with a sticky, bloody finger.

The girl panted like a dog. Watched him as he rose to stand in front of her.

Frank looked at the block and tackle. Followed the rope to where it was tied to a hook embedded in the floor. He clasped his hands in front of him. "I can't untie you yet," he whispered.

The girl took a breath, but Frank lunged forward and covered her mouth with his hand before she could protest. He put his lips next to her head. "Please. I *can't*. I can't alert those men in *any* way, you see? I'm going to kill them. Do you understand?"

She stiffened against him. He had no idea how old she was. How much of this she understood.

"Please," he repeated. "Do you understand?"

She nodded in his hand. He pulled his palm away from her mouth. She kept her lips closed, and Frank fell a long step away from her. Traced his way down the rope to the floor. Loosened the knot and gave her some slack. She sagged in relief as the pressure around her neck disappeared, and fresh tears rolled down to drop from the end of her nose.

Frank leaned back into her, and she put her face against his shoulder. "What's your name?" he whispered.

She swallowed. Tried to tell him. Cleared her throat softly. Swallowed again. "Jennifer," she said. Like the choking whisper of a ghost.

He couldn't breathe. Couldn't feel his extremities. Pain in his neck throbbed with his pulse, and the edges of his vision became a smoky gray.

He tried to swallow. It felt like there was wool in the back of his mouth.

Jennifer looked up, and her eyes searched his.

Narrowing in concern. Then alarm. Her hands were still bound, but she tried to turn. Rotate under the rope still going to the ceiling.

Frank got the lump down with a gasp. Shook his head. "No, no. Don't. Just wait for me here quietly, okay. Can you do that, baby?"

She bit her lower lip. Nodded her understanding.

Frank took slow breaths. Each one felt like fire. "How old are you, Jennifer?"

"My birthday was yesterday." Her voice still sounded like sandpaper.

"Happy birthday."

She smiled. Frank couldn't understand how she had the capacity. He felt blessed to have seen it. "Thank you," she whispered. "I turned thirteen. There was ice cream cake."

Frank's vision went from foggy gray to bloody crimson. The sizzling sound of static filled his ears. He put his hand on her cheek. Her tears mixed with Hines' blood.

"You have to be very quiet now, okay? I don't want these men to know what we're doing. And I don't want the police to show up before I'm done. Okay, baby?"

Jennifer nodded again.

Frank dropped his hand. Stepped to where he had placed his chain. Wrapped it back around his fist. Picked up his bloody weight. Noticed Hines staring up at him from the corner of his eye.

Frank dropped into a crouch that popped both of his knees. He balanced himself by setting the plate on the back of Hines' neck. "If you want to live, be in this exact spot when I get back. You even *blink* too many times, and I'll make it hurt. Nod if you understand."

Hines kept his eyes locked wide open. Nodded so hard, a fresh gout of blood splashed out from his eyebrow.

Frank walked to the door. The mounting sounds from

the other room told him that the girl was suffering. Had *been* suffering while he'd been taking his time.

Stupid, selfish old man.

He looked back over his shoulder. "I love you, Jenny."

He didn't wait to see if she heard him. He had work to do.

Chapter Seventeen

THERE WERE ONLY FOUR MEN. Either one had been a no-show, or he was taking a powder, and Frank would have to deal with him when he came up behind him later.

Frank didn't have time to wonder how he would handle it. His mind received a fresh blow of horror and outrage. He lost his breath two steps in.

One man lying back on a table covered with a pink beach towel. The little girl on top of him. Another man bent over her to sandwich her small body between them. Frank couldn't see their faces.

A third man off to the side. Frank recognized him from his image search. Detective Reed. He held the back of the back of the girl's head with both hands. Her forehead was pressed all the way to his flabby belly.

Like Jennifer, both hands were bound behind her.

The fourth man held a camera to his eye with one hand while stroking his glistening erection with the other. His name was Jacobs. A cop from Enola.

Frank had only action. Empty of thought and will as if his body moved on its own.

He stepped with his right foot to push off behind him with his left. Rotated like he was going to throw the weight plate for a gold medal.

It sliced through the air. Rising in an arc that brought the metal right into Jacobs' throat, its edge cutting through flesh. The momentum drove it through cartilage. The crunching snap of his windpipe tearing apart, and blood flung from the blow to splash the wall. Through the doorway to glitter in light from the hall.

Frank felt something pull in his side. A white-hot pain that radiated up into his ribs. Up under his collarbone.

Jacobs fell back with a choking gasp. Dropped his camera to smash on the floor. Raised his hands in the *I'm choking* gesture that nobody could address.

Crashed into the wall. His eyes were puzzled as he slid down to join the plastic shrapnel of the camera.

Frank's spin raised his rear foot, and he followed through with a savage knee to the cameraman's stunned face.

Teeth and nose crumbled. The back of his head punched through the plaster behind it.

Frank braced off the wall. Pushed back onto the room. Turned to find Reed had released the girl's head to stumble back in confusion.

The girl pulled in a wheezing breath, but she turned her head to vomit in the face of the man underneath her before she could scream.

Fresh guilt, but Frank couldn't help being relieved that she had remained quiet.

The man backpedaling away looked older than the others. He was a detective, so maybe a supervisor. Or an uncle. Frank didn't care.

Reed held his hands up in front of him. A sudden

supplicant. Frank had enough of his own prayers go unanswered to know how it felt.

He ducked into the man's guard. Drove his chained fist down to connect at the base of his softening penis. Frank cut Reed's choked howl short with a shoulder driven into the man's sternum. A knee driven up into the sagging testicles.

Reed fell to his knees, hands covering his crushed junk, and his mouth gaping in a silent scream. Frank fed him the weight.

Blood splashed up his forearm. Tiny spatters flying out when he drew his hand back for another shot.

Then a downward hook with the chained fist. Reed fell forward into a spreading pool.

Frank was gassed. He lifted his shoulders to draw a deep breath. Thanked GG for making him do the sprints. Cursed himself for all the drinking.

He turned back to find the man that had been the top bun of this sickening sandwich pulling back toward the neat piles of clothing along the wall. Holstered guns right on top. His name was Rosedale.

The bottom bun was Hernandez. Bucking his hips to get the girl clear as he swiped at the stringy puke on his face.

Frank was afraid the girl would tumble off and crack her unprotected skull, but he couldn't slow to help. He felt the pain in his side brighten to a spike that went across his lower back as he jumped past the table.

Lowered his shoulder and drove into Rosedale while bending to reach for the nearest weapon. Frank's shoulder met his hip, and they both went into the wall with jarring force.

The tip of Frank's head hit with a wet smack, and blood spilled from his split scalp. The top bun curled under him with a grunt. Worked to get his hands free. Rolling for position.

Frank wrapped Rosedale in a hug. One arm hooked under his leg. The other around his shoulders. He could feel the man's breath across his face.

Frank braced the way GG and Mo had shown him the first time he had tried to lift an Atlas stone. He had worked up to a 185-pounder before calling it quits.

Like riding a bike.

He braced with a deep breath. Thrust his hips forward and snatched the man away from the wall. At the top of the lift, Frank turned and raised his knees, putting himself on top as they dropped to the floor.

They landed with Rosedale's head underneath them. The crashing impact folded him, and Frank heard the snapping of bones.

The fall sent the weight from his hand, rolling away to spin on the floor like a giant coin. Frank struggled to stand. Wiped blood from his face in time to see the last man coming at him with wide open arms. Dripping penis bouncing with every step.

Right before Hernandez made contact, Frank wondered if the people downstairs were all looking up at the noise with puzzled curiosity.

Hernandez wrapped him up on impact. Lifted him as he drove toward the door. The back of Frank's head hit the top of the frame with a blinding crack.

Were they heading for the window?

He was answered by his back slamming into the wall between windows. Dust puffing out from the edges of the padded blanket.

Frank found himself on the floor. Sitting with his back against the wall, his feet splayed out in front of him. Hernandez stood over him with his hand pulled back for a serious punch. His lips were peeled back from his teeth. Little bits of vomit clung to his skin, trailing down his chest.

Frank focused on the flesh dangling in front of his face. Delicate and tender. Newly flaccid in the recent excitement.

Before the blow could land, Frank shot his hands up to grab the guy's slick garbage in a double grip. A frenzied pulling and tearing grip that brought an end to the man's heavyweight title aspirations.

His blows became fawning slaps. A panicked attack that had no chance of dislodging Frank. Hernandez fell to his knees. Battered on the top of Frank's head to get more blood flowing.

Frank whipped his head to the side to clear the flow from his eyes. Twisted and dug his fingers in.

The man's voice choked off into a whistling groan as Frank worked his feet under him. Drove Hernandez back. Held on as the man's writhing survival threatened to shake him loose.

Frank got his knees up, in spite of the torn muscle in his side waging a war of protest. Planted his foot on Hernandez' belly button. Jerked on his genitals like he was yanking a stubborn weed.

When he finally let go, Hernandez gasped through the spill of his *own* vomit, and his weeping followed Frank as he stumbled back into the room. The girl was on the floor under the table. Watching him on her side. Her gaze following him without blinking.

Reed, the chubby man who had tried to eat the weight, was still on the floor. Snorting through blood bubbles. Frank didn't think about it. He just dropped all of his weight into the knee he was already digging into the man's neck. A handful of seconds, and Reed barely struggled.

Just the weeping from the hallway. The sound of nails scraping on the floor.

Hernandez was trying to drag himself into the room, his gaze locked on the scatter of clothes where the guns had been. A trail of blood smearing behind him from his torn scrotum.

Frank stood with a wince. Limped past the man in the hallway. Turned with a sigh to lower himself on the man's back. Snaked an arm under Hernandez' throat. Locked in the chokehold and leaned back to squeeze as the agony in his abdomen ramped up to a blinding torment.

Hernandez finally stilled beneath him, and Frank rolled away to catch his breath. Massaged his side until he could force himself into a sitting position. Then onto his knees.

He made it back on his feet and into the room. The girl was sitting up, leaning against a table leg to watch him.

He bent with a groan to gather the first bit of cloth he could find. A cream-colored button down. He used the shirt to wipe as much blood from his face and head as he possibly could. Held pressure on the top of his head as he moved to the table for a towel.

He pulled the shirt away. Put a clean spot against his head. It came away with just a small spot and he threw it aside.

Frank looked at the little girl staring at him. Breathing through her open mouth.

"I killed them," he said.

Her eyes widened, and she nodded.

"I wish I could have been sooner. Or better ... I'm sorry."

The girl only stared.

He opened the towel to hold out in front of him. "I know I look a fright. Let me clean you up, baby."

At first, he didn't think she would come out from under

the table, but then she threw herself forward with a cry of despair. He caught her. Wrapped her in the towel. Rocked her until she finally calmed down.

Frank wiped her face with a clean corner of rough fabric. "Do you know Jennifer? The little girl in the next room?"

She shook her head.

Frank worked at the rope until he could finally free her hands. She hissed in pain as she brought them around, then threw them around his neck.

Like the Atlas stones, Frank braced again. Stood with her clinging to him. Limped into the other room where he found Jennifer standing in the same spot. She shivered as he approached. Stared at the little girl in his arms.

Frank stooped to let her stand on the floor, and for a cramping moment, he didn't think she would let go, but then she finally dropped.

Frank went to Jennifer. Untied her hands. Then the rope around her neck.

"Good girl," he said.

He turned to the other girl. "What's your name, sweetheart?"

She wiped her nose. "Becka."

Frank nodded. Turned his head to look for something he suddenly couldn't remember. He wanted to find their clothes. Wanted to finish up before that possible sixth man showed up. Wanted to …

His knees gave way, and he sat on the floor in a heap.

Jennifer hugged herself as a fresh chill went through her. Becka stepped close and opened her towel. Jennifer stepped in to press against her for warmth, and Becka wrapped them both.

They stood in each other's arms while Frank lowered his head and cried into his dirty hands.

Chapter Eighteen

NEITHER OF THE girls spoke as Frank cleaned up. They just sat side by side wrapped up in the pink beach towel. Watching him.

Jennifer's shivers had grown more violent and more frequent. Becka flinched every time she made a move.

Frank gave Hines petty punishments whenever he passed. A kick to the ribs. Digging his heel into the man's thigh. Stepping on him instead of around him.

He had all the men's belongings in a pile on the black tarp. Except for the guns. He added those to his backpack. He checked for clothes that fit to assemble a decent outfit that wasn't caked in drying blood and dust. Laced his shoes back up. Combed his hair with trembling fingers.

A bottle of water and a protein bar had helped to revive him. It seemed to help the girls too, but now they just sat with them sitting on the floor in front of them. The water and the bar both unfinished.

He squatted in front of them with a wince. "Okay, girls. I have to go outside for a second." They both rose in protest, and he lifted a forestalling hand. "I promise, just for a minute. I need to pull my van closer to the door. That's all."

Becka's gaze flickered over to where Hines lay on the floor.

Frank smiled. "I'll put him in the other room while I'm gone. You won't have to see him at all."

He could have had them move to one of the unoccupied rooms, but they seemed to be hanging on by a thread. He didn't know what any of this might do to them, and for the tenth time wondered if it would have been better if they hadn't survived this night.

He held up one finger. "Here. I'll show you."

He grabbed the length of rope Hines had used to tie Jennifer to the block and tackle. Ran it under Hines' knees. Stood to bundle both ends in his grip, then turned and hauled his body into the hallway. Around the corner to roll up against one of his dead friends.

Frank leaned back in. "See? Now … sit tight. I'll be right back."

He didn't wait for their response. Paused long enough to grab his tape, then went to the front room, taking a look over his shoulder before descending, as if expecting that sixth man to jump out of the corner.

He had gathered their cellphones. None of them seemed to be receiving messages or calls. Unless they were on silent mode. There were no sirens. Less noise from outside as the shops closed down.

Frank reached the bottom where it opened into a small lobby. A unisex restroom was right next to the front door. He went in, avoiding his reflection while washing his hands and face. Lathering and rinsing until the water ran clear. There were no towels. Only the wall-mounted blower, so he left while dripping all over the floor.

The side door Kirby used for his smoke breaks came

next. Frank went outside to breathe in the cool night air. A breeze chilling the water on his face. He pulled the door shut without latching it. Tore a hank of tape from the roll and stuck it over the lens of a camera installed beside the entry light.

Frank walked without hurry into the street.

Nobody was out behind the shops, and he drove his van onto the patio without incident. Parked with barely a gap between the van and the studio door.

He struggled to climb over his seat, then stepped on plastic stretched out in the van. Wriggled through the side door into the studio. Back up the stairs where he paused for a deep breath before finally going back into the room where he had left the girls.

They had gotten through their wait by getting dressed. He had found their clothes earlier. Offered them in a neatly folded pile. They had refused, burrowing deeper into the towel instead. He hadn't pushed it, but was happy to see them back in their clothes now.

He smiled as he entered, but they didn't smile back. Didn't react with relief. Only wide eyes.

Frank pointed to Jennifer, but looked into Becka's gaze. "Did you know it was her birthday yesterday?"

She shook her head, then turned to Jennifer. "Happy birthday for yesterday."

Jennifer smiled, and her teeth chattered in another shiver. "Thank you."

Frank slung his backpack up. Heavier with the guns. "I have to take this out, okay? I'll be back."

Jennifer lifted a shaking thumbs-up. Becka looked at it. Then she made the same gesture as if she'd just learned to do it.

Frank turned away before they could see him cry again. Took his time stowing the pack into the van and was panting by the time he got back upstairs. Curled over his side in pain.

He wanted to tell the girls a thousand things. Take them into his arms. Stroke their hair. Rock them until they fell asleep. But he couldn't.

He wiped his eyes before stepping back in for the final time. They were still side by side, but now more of the protein bar and water were gone.

"That's good. But there's still one last thing, okay? I have to get the men out of here."

Becka tipped her head, waiting for more, but Jennifer leaned forward. "Are you going to kill him too?"

Frank put a finger to his lip, but nodded with a smile. Jennifer did the same thing. Settled back against Becka. Pulled the towel higher on her shoulders.

"You're such good girls," Frank said.

He stepped backward into the hallway. Walked into the next room where he dropped down into a painful squat beside Hines. "I'm going to cut your feet loose because I'm not going to carry you. But I *will* shoot you without a thought after a second of trouble. In both knees. Then I'll put the barrel up your ass. Fire off another round. How's that sound?"

Hines nodded. Chuffed sound through the edges of the soaked tape keeping Jennifer's panties in his mouth.

Frank used his multi-tool to cut the zip-ties around Hines' ankles. Grabbed the man's shoulders and heaved him up on his knees.

He stepped back and dropped the multi-tool in his pocket. Drew the pistol from behind his back. "Get up. Let's get this over with."

Hines nodded with his hanging head. Like a horse looking for the oat bag. Grunted as he climbed to his numb feet, swaying once he was standing.

Frank stepped into the hallway. Motioned for Hines to follow. Kept him at an easy distance all the way down the stairs and over to the side door.

Hines balked at the plastic, but Frank was ready. Drove into his back so Hines' knees hit the lip of the step going into the van. He fell forward with a muffled shout.

Frank holstered the pistol. Jumped in to stand straddling Hines' squirming body. Hooked his fingers under the back of his waistband and pulled him inside. Turned to drop down and sit across his kidneys. Got his ankles again, then pulled them up for a party with the zip-ties, fixing them to the seat pedestal.

Frank shut the door, climbed back over the center console, and sagged into the driver's seat.

Hines struggled. Grumbled behind his gag. Frank ignored him as he started the van. Backed off the patio, then pulled into the alley leading to the street heading out of town.

He pictured the two little girls. Sitting in each other's arms in the middle of a bloody floor. Watching the door. Waiting for him to come back.

Another promise broken.

He pulled into the Walmart. In the shadows under a tree as far from the doors as he could get. Pulled the journal onto his lap. Turned on the light. Lifted his old phone and called 911.

A soothing female voice answered.

He took a calming breath. "I've killed four cops in Rosa Alta."

She tried to interrupt, but Frank talked over her. Telling her the address. Using the journal to deliver names for the dead policemen, then for the little girls those men had been abusing.

He told the dispatcher that they were good girls, and that they needed help.

She started to dig for more information, but he wouldn't let her finish. "I only have one more thing to say."

There was a moment of static-filled silence. "Go ahead, sir."

Her voice was calm — almost emotionless — but he knew her brain must be screaming. He had been in similar situations. Pretending to not let a sick criminal's confession get to him. Pretending that he didn't want to reach across the table and choke him to death.

"Sir?" the dispatcher said.

Frank smiled. "Just this. Tell Detective Bryan Owens I'm coming for him too."

These calls were recorded. If his message didn't get to Owens, it would get to someone who knew him. Or it would be kept from him. Frank didn't care.

He ended the call. Powered off the phone. Opened the door and slid out of the driver's seat to drop it on the ground. Then he kicked his phone under the back tire. Climbed back inside, and sat with his head tipped to the ceiling until the pain in his side finally eased enough for him to drive.

He rolled over the phone several times before pulling away. The sound of crunching under the tires was strangely satisfying.

Chapter Nineteen

IT WAS days before the pain subsided to the point where he could sleep comfortably. Walking the Playa Dolor sand with a bottle of bourbon. Drinking it straight. Not even returning the cork between hits.

He parked back under the carport next to the small building where Stan had stored the van in case things went south. Hines was a whining, stinking mess by then.

The building was a small pump house. A maintenance shed for the management of the beach. Frank didn't even know who maintained the place, but Stan had owned it, and a contractor came once a month to clean up the common areas.

The shed was clean and dry, though it smelled like rotten algae from the marshes. Frank pulled Hines out of the van. Let him fall on his face on the concrete.

Fresh blood worked under the edges of the tape, so Frank ripped it the rest of the way off. Hines rolled away as he cried out, and the soaked wad of Jennifer's panties fell from his mouth ahead of several bloody teeth.

He put his bruised cheek against the cool ground and lay still. Panting dust into the air.

Frank grabbed his toiletry bag from the back of the van. A clean beach towel. While Hines composed himself — or felt sorry for himself — Frank used a short hose attached to a corroded spigot on the wall to shiver through a cold shower.

Halfway through, he noticed Hines had rolled over and was watching him. Frank made eye contact while making sure he was thorough with his cleaning. Then he turned the cold water on Hines and watched him gasp and roll away, but he had nowhere to go to escape the spray.

Frank got tired of the game. Stopped to dry off. Tried to get a good look at the weeping cut on top of his head. Did a decent job with a wide bandage. Mostly bald skin anyway, making for easy adherence.

Finally, he grabbed a folding camp chair. Set it up several feet from where Hines had finally stopped squirming. Took his time getting the cooler out from behind the rear seat. Set the lid in his lap and laid out a nice meal for himself.

Turkey and pepperoni with moonshine mustard and muenster cheese on whole wheat bread. He almost stopped after making the second one. Decided he was going to need a third. Finished adding it to the sack, then he opened a beer and leaned back.

Took a bite and rolled his eyes with pleasure. Washed it down with half of his first beer. Looked at Hines with a raised eyebrow. "Now, then."

"Fuck you!"

Frank shook his head with reproach. Took another bite. Chewed slowly while Hines watched.

"What do you even want, man? The fuck are you?"

Frank wiped his mouth. Held up a finger while he took

another drink. Smacked his lips. "I just want some confirmation."

Hines tipped his chin up. "Can I have some of that?"

"Certainly." Frank grinned. "Just answer my questions."

"You ain't fucking asked me anything yet!"

Frank sighed. Leaned back to finish his sandwich in silence. Then the beer. He dropped the empty back in the cooler. Fished out a fresh one. Belched as he popped the top with the bottle opener on his multi-tool.

Hines made a desperate hop toward the chair. "Okay, okay. Just … can I have a little? Please?"

He set the lid aside. Stood with his multi-tool held out in front of him. "Do you remember what I told you last time?"

Hines nodded frantically. "Yeah, you said you'd put it up my asshole. Pull the trigger, I get it."

Frank nodded. Leaned over him to cut the tie holding his wrists and ankles together. Then he cut his hands free. Hines rolled over with a groan. Worked his hands in front of him. Looked down only to jerk back in horror. His fingers were swollen like inflated surgical gloves. Almost black. Blood wept from the shredded skin where the ties had been too tight. If there was such a thing.

Frank grabbed a handful of Hines' shirt at each shoulder. Pulled him up and dragged his body back to lean against the far wall. Walked back to the cooler. Opened a beer and walked back to set it on the ground next to Hines' knees.

"Be careful," he warned.

Hines nodded. Sniffed up a trail of snot. Wiped his eyes on his sleeve. He got the bottle between his puffy palms. Smiled in triumph as he pulled it up to suck on it noisily. As much spilled down his chin that went down his throat, but he seemed satisfied when letting the empty drop into his lap.

Frank sat back down. Rubbed the ache in his side. Aggravated when he yanked on Hines, but it still didn't seem as bad as he initially thought.

Hines rested his head back, eyes closed while Frank finished the other two sandwiches. Another beer for each of them. Then he cleaned up. Sat back in his chair with his journal.

"Now, then ..."

Hines cracked open one eye. Leaned forward to look down at his lap. "Go ahead."

Frank took out his pen. Put it next to the last name on his new Pedophile Junction list. "There was supposed to be a sixth man yesterday. What happened to him?"

Hines looked up. "Wilson?"

Frank looked at the name next to his pen. Lieutenant Carl Wilson. He nodded in confirmation. "That's right. Wilson."

Hines shrugged. "He got called in over lunch. Some bitch found a body in the restroom at the Golden Corral. Stabbed with one of the buffet knives."

"I see. But he would have been there otherwise?"

Hines gave a weak chuckle. "Oh yeah. He's a stickler for punctuality. Man of his word and all that. If Wilson says he's gonna do something, it's half done already. He's a freak about routines, too."

"Really?"

Hines' gaze flickered to the cooler next to Frank's chair. "Hey, can I have one of them sandwiches? You don't even have to make it for me, just ... a piece of cheese or something? I'm starving."

"As soon as we're done. You said Wilson is a man of routine?"

Hines sighed. Looked away. "Yeah." A ghost of a smile wrinkled the corners of his eyes before fading back into boredom. "He takes a shit the same time every day on his way to work. At the Home Depot in Enola. You could set your fucking watch by it. He must eat a lot of fiber."

Frank made a note. *Home Depot in Enola.* "And if I wanted to set my watch by it?"

Hines looked up in confusion. "Huh?"

"What time does he do this every day?"

"Oh. Two o'clock. Just before his shift at two-thirty."

Frank noted the new information. Closed the journal. "Thank you. *Now* we're through."

Hines' eyes narrowed in suspicion at Frank as he stood. "What's that supposed to mean?"

Frank loaded the cooler back into the van. Bagged up the dirty clothes and trash. Bundled everything inside.

"What's that supposed to mean?" Hines repeated with a shout.

Frank came back for his chair. "How did you pick her?"

"What? Who?"

"Jennifer."

"The fuck is that?"

Frank stood with the folded chair held against his waist. "You don't even know the name of the girl you were torturing?"

"That was *her* name? I never asked. Besides, she was Wilson's. I bet he was pissed when he got that call."

Frank clenched his teeth hard enough to shatter a molar.

He dropped the chair and Hines jumped in fear.

Frank walked over without a word. Hines flinched back again when Frank reached for him, but he only grabbed the bottle from Hines' lap. Pulled it up, turned it over in his hand, then smashed the glass onto the Hines' crown.

An empty *THUNK* followed by a squeal.

Again and again, until the bottle finally shattered.

Blood poured down in a crimson mask. Hines' pleading whine made bubbles form as it spilled across his lips.

Frank looked down at the jagged remains in his hand. He thought of driving it into the predator's neck, but he didn't want the mess. Plenty of blood was already staining the concrete in a pool underneath all the glittering broken glass.

Frank put the remains into the trash bag in the back. Pulled the duct tape out of his backpack.

Hines was desperate, lifting his hands in an attempt to ward him off, but Frank slapped them away. Pulled a strip away from the roll. Smashed it over his mouth. Pulled and pressed more and more of the tape to cover his face. Around and around his head. Layers and layers as Hines batted at his hands.

Frank finally stood, and Hines dragged his bloated fingers across the wet edges of tape. He sucked small gusts of air through the gaps. His eyes rolled in panic as he struggled to breathe.

Frank grabbed the bit of pant leg sticking out past the zip-tie around his ankle. Dragged his struggling body out of the pump house. Past the van into the gravel. Watched Hines work at the tape without progress. Glanced behind him to see where he was going.

The sun was starting to rise, spreading a pink glow to burn behind the clouds. A sight that would have made him pause a long time ago. Back when he'd been a different man.

He dragged Hines to the edge of some thorny bushes

where the ground grew soggy. The reeking of marsh was strong and biting.

Hines tried to wriggle away, but Frank moved to his side. Dropped into a squat. Put his hands on Hines' hip and pushed his body like a rolled-up carpet.

There was a moment of resistance, then Hines made it over the rise of the mud and weeds to flop down the concealed bank of an inlet feeding the pump house. With his feet bound and seven feet of tape wrapped around his head, Hines would drown in a couple inches of water.

The splash sounded deeper than Frank had expected.

And soon, the sounds of his struggles ceased. Frank turned away as the sun came out from behind the clouds. Like the sky was smiling on what he had just done.

Then a fresh cloud darkened the sky, and he was left with only his *own* smile.

It stayed there all the way back to the pump house until Frank looked down and realized he'd have to take another shower.

Chapter Twenty

EXCEPT FOR THE NIGHTMARES, his time on the beach did him good. The sweating regret he woke up with every night at odds with the light joy that had settled over his mind by day.

He couldn't listen to music through his Bluetooth adapter since destroying his phone on the trip back, so he listened to regular FM. When a commercial came on for a local store's big Halloween sale, he nearly swerved into oncoming traffic.

He had been so far out of reality, he didn't even know what *month* it was. Shocked that it was almost the end of October.

Freya had gotten out of school in early June.

He had lived entire lives in less than six months.

He wanted to pull over and count the days. Open an old paper calendar and tick them off one by one. This is when my house burned down. This is when my *other* house burned down.

Everything since Jenny had died — the collapse of his marriage, Sarah's suicide, getting out from under

Mallory Black's vendetta, killing Patrick Dahl ... all a blur.

It felt like twenty years ago since he had last seen his daughter's face.

He couldn't help smiling. A lightness was lifting him an inch from the seat.

The same satisfaction that had filled him when he killed before. Then the heat of guilt — not at the murders, but at feeling *good* about them.

And *still* he smiled.

He imagined Jennifer and Becka. In the arms of family. Or in the custody of a caring official organization. Then a cold shiver when his mind flashed on the memory of the ropes holding their hands behind their backs. The men and their cruelty. *Another* cop on the scene like them. Getting to the girls ahead of the paramedics.

The motion was suddenly nauseating.

His heart pounded. Pain lanced up under the left side of his jaw. His vision narrowed until all he could see was a bouncing dot of color in the center of his field of view.

A feeling of dread left a film of sweat across his forehead. With each exhalation, his voice was a keening fall.

He took his foot off the gas. Hit his flashers and drifted over to the side of the road.

A horn blasted as it passed. Then another as he drifted to a stop. Threw the shifter into *park*.

He was as bad as the men that had preyed on those girls. On *any* girls. What had he become?

He wasn't an avenger. A protector. He was a cold-blooded murderer. A vigilante that had damned his soul nearly six months ago.

His anxiety faded in breathless relief. Like a coach doused with Gatorade on the sidelines.

Jennifer and Becka were *not* fine. He had saved them in

the moment, but there were years of trauma ahead of them. But still, there was a chance, because of him. In this case, a chance was all he could ask for.

His daughter no longer had one, but there was a chance he could still find her killer. Exact his revenge on her behalf, whether she would want it or not.

He put the van back in gear. Looked over his shoulder for a gap in traffic.

A man couldn't go to hell *twice*.

The smile was back before Frank recovered his speed, pulse still throbbing on the side of his neck, but the nausea was gone. He could finally get a full breath.

His side barely hurt, and he would be home in more than enough time to get drunk while watching the sunset. Maybe he'd even grill some salmon.

THE EVENING HAD BEEN DREAMY, but the night was dreamless.

He slept in. Waking late to the sounds of cars driving over gravel. He took his time with his coffee. A long shower. When he was done, the weekly meeting was already underway.

He made another cup of coffee — his third or fourth, he wasn't sure. Added a dash of brandy. Sat at the top of the steps to listen, but Rogers' voice seemed more condescending than usual.

The rapt attention of the participants seemed overly zealous. Like they were all waiting for a comet to gaze upon with their Kool-Aid.

He carried his coffee down the stairs. Avoided eye contact while passing through. Out in the yard he paused to watch Gen push a sled through the dirt next to the side fence.

He didn't think she was still trying for a state record of any kind, but she was working with the same obsessed passion he remembered from his previous life.

He looked at the back of the house. Decided to take advantage of Mo and Gen being otherwise occupied. Walked all the way to the front porch. Into the chill air inside.

His smile slipped as he turned the corner into the kitchen, but he had it back on by the time he stepped into GG's room.

Frank thought he was sleeping. Stood back against the wall to watch GG in a moment of peace.

"Hey, Dad," GG said. Squinted up at Frank with a smile.

Frank shook his head as he walked around the bed. Sat in the chair and leaned back to cross his legs. Took a loud sip of his cooling coffee.

GG closed his eyes and settled back into his pillow. "You doing what you're supposed to?"

Frank tipped his head. "Yes and no."

"Oh yeah?"

Frank set his cup on the small table next to GG's bed. "Well, I did the sprints, but my diet has been admittedly poor."

"How poor?"

"And I spent a lot of time on the beach. Swimming and drinking. Taking notes in my van."

GG turned to look at him. "What have you been up to?"

Frank told him. Every detail.

When he was done, GG asked the question he had been ignoring all day. "You think them girls are okay?"

"I don't think they'll *ever* be okay."

"That's not what I mean. Are they okay *now*?"

Frank sighed. "I don't know."

"You shouldn't have left 'em."

"Maybe."

"You can't trust anybody."

"Probably."

The morphine dispenser bubbled in the sudden quiet. GG reached up to wipe the sweat from his forehead. Frank wondered how it didn't just freeze on his skin given how cold it was in the room.

"I went to the doctor," GG said.

Another thing Frank wanted to ignore. "Yeah?"

"Yep. I got a couple weeks maybe. Month at the most."

Did he mean a couple weeks since two weeks ago when he went? Or from now? Frank didn't know what to say, and the silence stretched out like static.

The morphine bubbled again. The doses seemed much closer than they used to be. Frank grabbed his coffee to hide behind the rim as he sipped. Cold and bitter, and the brandy tasted like sour honey.

"He said it would get a lot worse before the end," GG whispered.

"I'm sorry," Frank muttered around his cup.

"Me too. It already hurts so bad."

"I'm sorry," Frank repeated.

"You think about what I asked?"

Frank closed his eyes. Kept his mouth shut.

"Come on, Dad. I don't want to finish my life out the way it looks like it's gonna. I'm wearing a fucking diaper."

Frank looked out the window, but the curtains were closed. He stared at the glowing fabric. "Why me?"

GG sighed in disgust. "You don't think I ain't asked somebody else? Gen just cries. Busts out and runs away."

"And Mo?"

"He won't even argue. Just stares with lips pressed together like he's getting ready to play the trumpet."

"Fine," Frank said.

"Fine what?"

"I'll do it."

Frank hadn't been sure what his answer would be until he said it. Could doing this terrible thing in the name of mercy redeem him at all? He didn't think so. But there still wasn't a reason *not* to.

"You will?" GG said, and his face opened in a half-grin. Tears rolling from his good eye. His other one stared dumbly from under his sagging brow. "When?"

"I got a couple things to finish first. And then I'll do it. I promise."

"You promise?"

"I do."

The morphine bubbled.

Frank jumped in alarm when the front door opened. He didn't know how long he'd been sitting there listening to GG's pump.

He heard Gen humming under her breath as she went deeper into the house. He didn't want to confront her right now. He looked down at GG to let him know he was leaving, but his eyes were closed again. Lips puffing out with his breath.

Frank stood with as little sound as he could. Hustled out before Gen could catch him there.

An odd thought. Like he was doing something wrong.

He sighed in relief when he made it out to the front porch.

When he got back to the barn, the session was breaking up. He refused every effort to engage him, weaving through the crowd to the stairs. On his way up, he caught

Mo watching him with disapproval. Shaking his head before turning his back.

Instead of lacing his coffee, Frank went with straight brandy in his cup. Looked around like a man trying to find his glasses only to discover they were on his head.

It was his phone that he wanted. Then he remembered crushing it in the Walmart parking lot. Begrudgingly, he picked up the new phone that Stan had sent. Powered it up and waited.

Sure enough there were messages. All from Stan. Mostly chiding greetings, but the last two were of interest. A link to a recording under the text, *You've made an impact.*

A link to another recording under the text, *Not as much as you think.*

Before clicking the first one, he scrolled back to make sure nothing was there except for, *Turn your phone on bitch,* and, *Technology will set you free.*

If his phone was off, how was Stan expecting him to get those messages? He rolled his eyes as he clicked the first link. Held the phone's speaker to his ear.

Muffled voices and static, then the recording resolved into the middle of a conversation.

"I'll take care of it," said a voice.

A decent recording, despite the distortion. Good enough to know the voice belonged to Bryan Owens.

"It looks like *we'll* be taking care of it." Frank didn't recognize the second voice at all. "Just be thankful I was so close. Be thankful I was *listening.*"

"I said I'll take care of it."

A loud sigh. "Frank Grimm made a mess …"

More static and muffled voices.

"… sure you get put away in Santa Rosa where you'll die in a fucking riot, but not before you get fucked bloody, you hear me?"

Owens growled. "Be careful how you speak to me."

"Don't act like you got something over me, son."

"Be careful how you speak to me!"

The audio clipped into distortion. Settled back into muffled confusion. Cleared on the second voice.

"One way or the other, this will end. Senator Mickelson was coming next week, for fuck's sake!"

"I don't care about your senator," Owens said.

It didn't surprise Frank that a senator was involved. *Nothing* could surprise him about the evil men were capable of.

"I only care about Frank Grimm, and then getting back to normal."

"So, we agree on *something*?" the second voice said.

The silence stretched out for so long, Frank thought the recording was over. Then Owens said, "I guess we do."

How had Stan gotten this?

What did it mean?

Frank clicked the second recording. It was Ty Kirby's podcast. Frank looked down at his watch in confusion. The podcast was from this afternoon. How could he be recording in that studio? Why hadn't the cops shut him down?

Frank stopped the recording.

He saw Jennifer and Becka hugging each other under the towel. Looking up at whoever came through the door when Frank never came back.

Chapter Twenty-One

THERE WAS something about a Saturday morning hangover that Frank enjoyed. The thought that there were two days to recover if one were returning to work on Monday. Or two days to make it worse if one wasn't.

He kept his body as busy as he could to keep his mind from settling on his dread. Forced himself to hit a slow five miles out on the road. Washed the van inside and out. Burned the dirty clothes from last week. Boxed up the guns.

Every time Frank walked past his phone, he picked it up to see if there was a new notification, but it remained blank.

He worried about the ache in his side. It seemed so hot and swollen. Like there was a problem deep inside. It was only hurting, so he tried to dismiss it.

But like the dread building in the back of his mind, the pain wouldn't leave him alone.

He took his time cleaning himself up in the afternoon. Paid extra attention to trimming his goatee. Some pomade in his hair to comb it straight back. Little curls at the ends at the base of his skull.

A T-shirt under his usual tropical button-down. He kept the cargo shorts and flip-flops, though.

He tucked one of the pre-made meals under his arm. Cod and rice. Pulled a bottle of wine from the cooler. A red Pimler that would have been right at home in Carmen's hand.

Best not to think of that. He grabbed the corkscrew on his way out. Walked to Gen and Mo's front door as the sun sank behind the trees to drape the yard in azure shadows.

He took a deep breath and knocked on the front door.

Soft steps let him know it wasn't Mo answering the door. Gen's face looked out in caution, then lit with an open grin that surprised Frank so much, he nearly burst out crying.

She flung the door open and danced onto the porch. Moving her muscular body in the mincing steps of a much smaller woman. And she was in his arms.

He was so sick of the tears. Of losing control. But the sound of her crying in his ear eroded his resolve. He didn't even know what they said to each other. Just the sounds of the words.

The *feelings*. Regret. Apology. Forgiveness.

He had been so scared that it would be awkward. Painful to be around them. No matter how he tried, he couldn't avoid their acceptance.

Knowing he didn't deserve what he had made it harder to take, but this night wasn't for him.

He passed her the bottle of wine. She apologized for not making enough for him too. He displayed his container of food. Asked to use her microwave. She laughed and took the container with a scolding wag of her finger.

"My man!" Mo shouted, and for a moment, Frank was

back at Wild One, swallowed in a killer bear hug. And for a while, things were good.

Frank suspected they could feel what was under the surface just like he could. But if they were willing to put it all aside for the sake of a nice family dinner, he could keep it together. Leaning in and including GG for a soft moment. Leaving him to his rest.

Then it came time for dessert.

Chocolate pie.

Gen cut a generous piece. Laid it on a small paper plate. Folded napkin. Plastic fork over the fold. "It's the only thing he can still taste. The only thing he tries to keep down."

Frank looked at the other paper plates sitting empty. "Should we take ours in there? A little picnic around his bed?"

She grinned with tears in her eyes. "He would love that."

With pie in hand, they filed in to find GG sitting up. Wide-eyed and waiting. "Thanks, Genny!" He held out his good hand to take the plate.

Frank's heart jolted at the sound of his daughter's name, then again when GG looked at him with a warm smile. "Hey, Dad. I missed you."

"Me too."

GG laughed. "What, you missed *yourself*?"

Mo laughed as he crowded in next to the bed, shrinking the room with his bulk.

There was small talk and laughter. Gen sat at GG's side. Helped him guide the fork in. Dabbed at chocolate on the corner of his mouth. Brown foam forming in his sagging lips.

Mo gathered the plates when it was over. Stood with his chest expanded in pride. "This was real nice."

"Yeah it was," GG said. "For the last time we did it, I'm glad it was so good."

"Greg!" Gen shouted. Whiffed a little slap at his wrist. "Don't talk like that."

Frank crossed his arms. "Why not?"

She looked up at him like he was too stupid for such a simple concept. "Because …" She fell silent as she sat back.

Frank sighed, looking at GG as she held his gaze with a smile. "He doesn't want it to end the way the doctors told him it *would*."

Gen put her fists on her thighs. "But that's—"

"Gen," Mo said. Voice soft but firm. Like a diesel engine warming up in the winter. "Honey, he's been talking about it for weeks."

She pursed her lips. "Talking about what?"

Frank put his hands in his pockets. Kept his gaze locked on GG's. "He asked me to kill him before the pain is too much. Before he forgets who we are. Before he forgets who *he* is."

Like it was making his point, the morphine pump kicked in.

Gen covered her mouth and looked away.

Frank leaned forward and put his hands on the lower railing of GG's bed. "I'm going to do it, too."

GG's face twisted along with her erupting sob. He buried his face in his good hand and cried.

"When?" Mo asked.

"Soon. But not while you're here."

Gen slapped her thigh. "Are we serious here? Are we really talking about this? *Killing* a man?"

Frank grunted. "It's easier than you think."

Gen jumped up and pointed her finger at GG. "He's a *good* man, Frank. You're talking about killing a good man, not some ..." She spread her hands, looking for the word. "Murderer."

Frank smiled and stood up straight. "But that's what I am. Kill a good man or a bad man, you're still a murderer."

She dropped her hands. Marched toward him only to stop just shy of touching him. "Get the fuck out of my way." She took a deep breath. "Please."

Mo and Frank pressed themselves back. Lifted their hands to let her pass. She stormed into the kitchen where she began aggressively cleaning up dinner.

Frank looked at Mo. "I wonder if she knows how lovely she is."

Mo shrugged. "I ain't sure."

"Do you tell her?"

"Every day."

Frank grinned. "My man."

GG sniffed. Wiped his eyes. "When are we doing it, Dad?"

Frank raised his eyebrows at Mo. "Can you two take a trip? Start early?"

Mo looked pained. "Not too early. I'm getting that new gray water tank put in. Maybe not until late Wednesday."

Frank nodded. Turned to GG. "How about that, buddy. We'll have a nice long weekend together."

"Then you'll do it?" GG whispered.

"Yes. Then I'll do it."

"That sounds just fine."

The morphine pump kicked in with its gurgle.

Frank almost laughed at the timing, then he sobered when Gen was back in the doorway. Face red and swollen. Eyes puffy. "If you're really going to do this, I'll need to show you how."

Frank suddenly realized he hadn't considered his methods. The image of him holding a pillow over GG's face flashed through his mind, and he shook his head. He thought about all the guns he had stashed in a mailbox out in the barn.

He looked from GG to Gen. "Okay. How?"

She crooked her finger. "Come in here. I don't want him hearing."

"Aw, come on," GG whined.

Gen shook her finger at him. "Mind your business, Greg, and I'll bring you another piece of pie."

GG ducked his head. "Yes, ma'am."

She turned back into the kitchen without looking back. Mo shrugged as he followed her out. Frank brought up the rear, but froze at the door when GG grabbed him in his iron grip. Tingling pain radiating up his forearm.

"I love you, Dad," GG said.

"I love you too, buddy."

GG nodded. Let go and eased back into bed.

Frank rubbed the spot where GG had grabbed him. Bruises from the last time he had his fingers dug into his arm probably weren't even faded. He shook his head in wonder at the strength still in that dying body as he joined Gen at the island.

A scattering of papers was in front of her. She sniffed and reached for the top of the pile. Lifted a brochure up in front of him. "This is his morphine pump."

Frank wiped his eyes and nodded. "Okay."

She opened the brochure. "It has a purge function. Where the pump comes on and runs cleaning fluid through the system. But there's a failsafe, right?"

Frank nodded. "So people don't blast a patient with a gallon of morphine."

"It wouldn't take that much, but yes, that's essentially why."

Mo was busy throwing the paper plates away. Washing the forks from dessert. But Frank could tell he was paying attention.

"It needs to have the line plugged back in to the top here," Gen continued. "So there's a loop. Then it discharges through a drain line in the bottom. *But*, if you make it think the line is looped back in, you can start the purge cycle."

"I see." Frank didn't *really*, but he figured there would be time for questions later.

"That's why you need this." She held up a little crook of metal wire.

"A paperclip?"

"That's right." She nodded. "There's a reset button behind a little hole on the top. You jam this in and depress the button. After it resets, you keep the paperclip pushed in, and start the purge cycle."

Frank looked at the pictures. Saw the hole. He took the brochure from her hand. "I understand."

She pointed the paperclip at his face. "You have to be there the whole time. Do you understand *that*? Until it's over. You have to be there … watching."

Frank took the paperclip. "I understand."

"Good," she said.

"How did you figure this out?"

"You weren't the only one he asked."

She stomped off and Mo followed her.

Frank let himself out.

Chapter Twenty-Two

FRANK SPENT Sunday on the road. Driving back to Rosa Alta.

He listened to the entire Ty Kirby recording, and it was business as usual. The only mention of *anything* out of the ordinary was Kirby's report about a listener "swatting" him.

A disgruntled ex-fan called in a report to the police that ended up with the SWAT team pounding at his door. "Maybe you know this, but I have friends in high places. To anybody else who might try this, it won't go unnoticed or unpunished."

Frank couldn't help feeling like Kirby's statement was directed at him.

He cruised by his usual parking spot. Along the storefronts to where the studio was.

Everything seemed perfectly normal. He even choked on laughter at the sight of duct tape still flapping on the camera lens next to the side door.

He could probably go up the metal stairs to the rear door and find it unlocked.

Had it happened the way he remembered?

Of course it had.

Then Frank thought about what GG had asked. If he really believed those two girls were really safe. His fingers tightened on the wheel. Yes, he *had* to believe it.

A slow loop around the block, and he parked by the dumpsters. Spent the day at the beach. Pushed through the tourists for a burger and a beer at a bar called Whendango! A guy with a guitar and a stomp box belted out old bluesy folk, and Frank enjoyed himself in spite of trying his best to manage the opposite.

He only deserved pain.

He rolled his eyes at his own dramatic self-hatred. He was growing tired of manufacturing new ways to loathe himself.

Back in the van under the far tree in the Walmart parking lot — he even saw tiny glittering bits of his smashed cell phone on the ground — Frank scrolled through a website about building a kegerator out of an old freezer. Finally kicked on his little fan and lay back. The last thing he remembered was telling himself there was no way he was going to fall asleep.

He went to Sammy's diner in the hopes of seeing her again, but instead his server was a bored young man named Chad. Black glasses, tight black jeans, and derisive smile.

Chad only got ten percent.

Frank consulted his watch. Then his digital map. Enola was right next to Rosa Alta. They had a small brewery open early for lunch. He could take his time getting there, enjoy a sandwich and a cold brew, and be at the Home Depot just in time.

The sky was a beautiful clear blue. The sun bright and clear, but not balefully hot. A nice mid-autumn breeze blowing his hair back. He sat on the patio with his lunch. Ate everything, even the pickle. Had two of their house stouts before rolling out.

The ache in his side was a dull spread of pain that he could ignore, but as soon as he focused on it, another fifteen minutes would go by before he could start to forget it again.

He pulled in to the Home Depot parking lot with fifteen minutes to spare. He had no idea what kind of car he was looking for, but he would recognize Wilson when he got there, so he left the van and went in to look up at the signs hanging from the ceiling. Like a shopper trying to find the right aisle.

The restroom sign caught his eyes. An arrow pointing him to the back of the store. The multi-tool in his cargo pocket bounced with his steps.

He walked into the men's room as a kid in an orange apron came out of the nearest stall. Buckled his belt and smoothed his apron before washing his hands.

He caught Frank's eye in the mirror. "How you doing, chief?"

Frank gave the kid a salute before turning into the second stall. "I'm doing well, and you?"

"Can't complain," the kid said over the sound of the water in the sink.

Frank waited for him to finish washing his hands. Gritted his teeth when it went on for far too long. The kid had a stain or he was just *very* thorough.

The jet engine inside the hand dryer blasted off, and the kid went through two cycles before finally walking out.

Frank left his stall to stand in front of the sink. His pulse pounded in his neck. Sweat beaded on his forehead. From the corner of his eye, he saw a shadow enter the restroom. He bent over to turn on the water as somebody came in. Frank glanced up. Kept his gaze at chest level. Right across Wilson's gray tie.

Frank looked back at his hands. Kept them out of the water while pretending to wash them. Wilson passed in a wave of overpowering aftershave. Whistling through his teeth. Sport coat draped over his arm.

Of course he would go to the handicap stall.

Frank shut the water off as the stall door closed. Then he stepped up to the dryer.

The sound of Wilson's belt buckle. A jingle of keys as he lowered his pants. Frank hit the button on the dryer.

He rushed to the stall next to Wilson as a heated bray filled the restroom. Pulled the multi-tool out. Opened it to a serrated blade.

He eased the door closed behind him. Stepped up on the toilet rim and dropped into a half squat. Looked up at the top of the stall. It seemed so far away.

The ringing music of a mobile game killed the silence as the dryer died. A gassy fart. The splash of some business taking place.

Frank pushed with both feet as he hooked his free hand over the metal wall. Halfway through, his right knee hit the edge, and instead of carrying over in a spinning jump that would see him landing on his feet in a superhero crouch, he rolled over the top like a flopping bag of oatmeal.

Fortunately, there was a shocked officer to break his fall.

He landed curled up in Wilson's lap. The phone flew out of the stall to slide out of sight. The toilet flushed under them as Wilson threw himself back in alarm, then a bellow of pain as all of Frank's weight pushed his back into the chrome plumbing.

"What the fu—"

Frank's knife was at his throat.

He balanced on Wilson's knees with one toe stretched out to keep from falling. His other foot planted flat against the sidewall. He grabbed a handful of gray tie for added leverage.

The ripping pain in his side felt like a burning splash of acid.

He forced himself into a new position. Working through his own winces of pain. Through Wilson's twitching discomfort. He finally found a position next to the toilet and held onto the metal rail bolted to the wall.

"Okay." Frank offered his victim a nod.

"What do you want?" Wilson demanded, too loud.

Frank flinched back from the volume. "Keep it down, Wilson. You wanna bring the whole store in here?"

His eyes narrowed. "How do you know me?"

"I missed you last Friday. I had a lot of fun in Rosa Alta."

Wilson stared, his right hand resting on his belly. A millimeter closer to the holster under his opposite arm. "If that was you, then you are fucked, my friend."

"Like the friends you abandoned?"

Wilson shook his head. Bared his teeth when the movement made the knife bite into his skin. "What do you think happened there? What were you trying to do, save those girls?"

Frank shrugged.

Wilson smiled. "What's your name? Frank Grimm, right? Trying to save those girls like you saved your daughter?"

Frank refused to take the bait. Pressed the knife in a little harder. "Just keep still. You think I can't see you turtling your hand across your fat gut? In fact—"

Frank darted his hand forward. Popped the snap and pulled the pistol. Put it up under Wilson's chin.

Wilson lifted both hands out to his side.

Frank smiled in triumph. "So, I want Owens."

"I don't care."

"What?"

Wilson smiled. "I don't give a shit what you want. The people I'm involved with are bigger than both of us. Now that I'm in this, I can never get out. I know too much. Just like Owens."

Frank shook his head. "I don't understand. "

"I know. And it's fucking sad."

"Fine. Then what happened to Jennifer and Becka?"

"Who?"

Frank pressed in against him. Pushed the barrel up into the flesh under Wilson's jaw. "The girls I rescued."

"The girls you rescued? You didn't rescue *shit*. I got here first, dumbass. Handled the scene before anybody else showed up."

Frank's mind was a dying animal. Broken and torn. His thoughts were the flies swarming around the wounds.

He drove Wilson back. Put one foot on the locked door behind him for something to push against. His elbows dug into Wilson's soft chest.

Wilson's strangled cry became a shocked gasp. He thrashed, but Frank held him down. Heard the crunch of breaking bone. Felt warmth on his hand. Held his breath and pushed until his vision blackened with effort.

He stood panting in front of Wilson's knees as his vision resolved back into bright color. His right hand was covered in a slick of blood, but it was empty. His left hand still held the gun.

He looked at Wilson to see the multi-tool handle protruding from a gory tear in his swelling neck. A faint drip of blood falling in a pool spreading back into the corner where the floor sloped into a drain.

Frank looked up at the top of the stall. It seemed even farther than he remembered.

He dropped down to roll under the gap between the stall and the floor. Back into his own stall where he stood in confusion. Like he couldn't remember how he got there.

He dropped the pistol in his cargo pocket where its weight tried to pull his shorts down.

Out to the row of sinks where he washed his hands longer than the Home Depot kid had earlier. He looked up at himself in the mirror. His hands were clean, but there was blood all over his shirt.

He spun away with his palms out. Flung water on the metal doors behind him. He rushed to Wilson's stall. Rose on his tiptoes and reached over the top. Felt around until his fingers found the sport coat hanging on a hook by the door.

He whipped it over and shrugged into it. Passed by the dryer as he buttoned it up. Stepped into the treated lumber aisle. Walked with his hands in his pockets all the way back to his van.

Chapter Twenty-Three

FRANK DROVE without paying attention to where he was headed. Barely aware of other vehicles. His hands and feet going through the motions.

When he became aware again, he looked up to see Ty Kirby's studio slide by.

He got the impression it wasn't the first time he'd passed the place.

He took one more circuit. Unable to make a decision about his next move.

He finally pulled into his spot beside the dumpster. Killed the engine without lowering the windows, then struggled over his armrest to climb past the center console. Back into the dim interior where he flung Wilson's jacket off. Tore the buttons off his shirt to pull it loose. Fought to shake it free, sitting in the floor between the middle seats, scrubbing at the blood drying in the wrinkles around his wrists.

Like cuffs encircling his hands. Holding him to his deeds.

He cried until his throat ached. His side burning in

wave after wave of spasms. His heart beat so hard, it made him rock on his knees. He could almost hear its echo.

He dug into his cooler. Washed his hands and arms with ice. Dragged the rough melt across his face and chest. Until his skin was red and raw. He sat back on his heels and closed his eyes. Bounced with his pulse. Wondered if he had ruined the new carpet with all the water.

He climbed back in the driver's seat. Watched the people on the beach. The ones on the sidewalk behind him across the street. Living and loving and having fun right next to a building where terrible things had happened. Things that would probably happen again.

How many tourists walked through Oklahoma City without sparing a thought for the children gone?

Frank suddenly hated them. Every person he saw. Especially anyone that smiled. He thought about driving into the sand. Striking every one of them that didn't get out of the way in time. Up on the sidewalk and into the front windows of the shops beneath the upper floor.

He started the van. Rolled the front windows down. Leaned into the open as he backed out. Joined the lazy traffic and steered toward home.

Every few minutes, a child's face would go through his head. Jenny. Rory Day. Freya. Jennifer and Becka.

He had saved one. At the expense of his own soul, and it had been worth it. The terrible guilt that gnawed at him. The ugly person he had become. Treating himself as bad as he could manage. Nowhere near the suffering of any of those girls.

He picked up his phone. Thought for a moment about calling Freya. Just to hear her voice again. To prove that he actually *had* done one good thing in his life.

He dropped the phone back into the tray on the center console with a growl. It would have been better if he'd died trying to save her. If he and Dahl had killed each other.

But then he never would have killed Briar.

But then he never would have failed Jennifer and Becka.

Frank slammed his hands on the wheel. He didn't *know* that they hadn't been found by paramedics after the 911 call.

Wilson said he had gotten there first.

But he could have been lying.

Until Frank drove by and saw for himself.

He shook his head. What had he actually seen? Just because there weren't any police there now didn't mean there hadn't been any a week ago.

But there wasn't any yellow tape. And Kirby was still podcasting.

Nothing said he was recording in *that* building still.

Frank felt his belly gurgle. Hunger twisted a knot in his guts. Burned up into his throat. He looked up and saw a Sloppy's. Veered onto the exit without his usual rationalization.

He wanted garbage, and a lot of it.

The drive-thru menu board advertised a *SCARY GOOD DEAL* of buy one meal, get the second half-off. Frank picked two numbers at random. It felt like each bag weighed five pounds.

He ate while driving. Juggling sauce and fries and Dr. Pepper. Going through napkins like a man missing his bib at a lobster-eating contest.

When the phone buzzed, he looked out both windows in confusion before realizing what it had been.

He divided his attention between the road and the screen. Keeping the van as straight as he possibly could.

Intent on occupying his mind with more than doubt and anger.

You're being followed.

He dropped the phone back. Kept himself from wheeling around to get a look. The rearview mirror was practically useless. He always drove with the curtains down to obscure the interior. He may as well have been driving a windowless panel van.

The side mirrors were food for navigation, but difficult to spot details. He needed to get off the interstate so he could pay more attention.

He made sure to signal with plenty of time. Checked both sides for followers. He exited again and three cars followed. His fingers fed fries into his mouth without benefit of thought. Just grab and chew until they were gone.

A brown sedan. A green pickup. A blue hatchback.

Frank pulled into a Sunoco station next to a Taco Bell. He paused when he looked down to realize he had no shirt. Then he shrugged. This was Florida.

Sure enough, nobody looked at him twice as he perused the wire rack full of snacky-cakes. Kept his eye out the front window for any of his three pursuers.

The brown sedan won as it pulled into one of the far pumps. Frank grabbed a bag of coconut-covered donuts and noticed nobody got out to pump any gas.

He tore it open before getting back to the van. Had two of the little doughnuts in his mouth before starting back up.

He didn't pay much attention to the brown car the rest of the way home. Just a glance up here and there to make sure they were still behind him.

Sometimes directly. Other times with a car or two between them, but always there.

As he got closer to home — to the fields and back roads, Frank noticed the car staying farther back. Sometimes losing sight of it altogether. But he didn't want that — he needed them to know where he lived.

Turning onto his own road, Frank caught the flash of the sun reflecting off the front bumper. Took it nice and slow to the gravel drive leading him to the rear of the barn.

He turned in, and was pulling into the lane that wrapped around to the wide doors just as the car passed by. He knew they wouldn't just tear down the driveway, guns blazing.

They would find the route to the front of the property. Get a lay of the land. So they could plan.

Frank parked inside. Jumped out and made his way into the yard. Keeping a casual eye on the road.

Mo was next to the RV. Tools scattered. The wide access panel leaning against the nearby shed. He stood with sweat dripping down his chest like an ad for cologne.

"You done already?" Frank shouted.

Mo looked down at his watch. Then back up with a confused smile. "*Already?* It's been all day."

Frank nodded. Looked over Mo's shoulder. "Yeah, but are you done?"

Mo nodded. "Except for the cleaning up, I think so."

Frank leaned against the side of the RV. Crossed his arms. "So was that the last thing?"

Mo narrowed his eyes. "Yeah. Why?"

Frank shrugged. "Just wondering."

The brown sedan appeared at the edge of the property. Not driving too slow, or barreling along at the area's typical breakneck speed. Even the mailman roared down the road as if making a time trial.

Frank shifted his gaze to Mo as the sedan drove by. "How long will it take to pack?"

Frank pushed off the RV to watch as the sedan faded down the lane.

Mo spun to see what Frank was looking at, but the car disappeared at the stop sign with a turn. He pulled a small towel from his waistband. Scrubbed at his hands and wiped it across his chest. "What's going on, Frank? What have you brought to my house?"

Frank didn't want to lie anymore, so he told Mo about what had happened at Home Depot. When he finished, Mo stood with his hands at his sides. Staring open-mouthed like he couldn't get enough air. So Frank told him how he had ended up at Home Depot in the first place.

The sun was dipping low by the time he finished. His throat was dry and his eyes burned from suppressing his tears. He heard a small choking behind him. Spun to see Gen standing there with a hand over her mouth. Face slack with horror.

He wondered how much she had heard. If she now thought he was the monster all along. She shook her head as she came to him with open arms.

He couldn't believe it. How could she do this after what he had said? He fell into her, and she held him as he cried.

Mo's big hand put heat on his shoulder. Hot breath in his ear. "It ain't your fault, man."

But Frank knew better, and it only made him cry harder.

They offered him dinner. A drink on the porch. He declined. Mo nodded. "That's probably best. It looks like we need to pack."

Gen touched his cheek and opened her mouth to say something, but she shook her head and stepped back. "We'll talk in the morning."

He watched them walk away. In step and leaning into each other.

Back at the barn, he wasted no time opening a bottle of tequila. Two ice cubes dropped into a glass. He went out to sit on his balcony, and as he raised the glass to his lips, Frank saw the sedan parked at the edge of the neighboring field.

He barely registered the vehicle's presence before it drove away.

Chapter Twenty-Four

FRANK TOLD himself he would be ready for anything, but fell into that bottle with his usual abandon. Drink after drink while watching the road in front and behind.

The bottle returned the favor, though.

He held it against his chest as he staggered to bed. Tipped it over his melting ice cube on the bottom of his glass. Frowned in disappointment when only a few drops came out.

He managed to get the glass to his nightstand, but then his knees gave way, and he planted his face in the comforter. The bottle slid from his fingers to the floor. Rolled in a long spiral with a musical ring. Frank heard music as he fell asleep.

Snatches of dreams about listening to the radio in the van as cops chased him out of Rosa Alta. All the girls he couldn't save were in the seats behind him. The passenger seat was empty. That had upset him for some reason.

Then he dreamed of the floor creaking underfoot as he tried running down the hall to save Jennifer and Becka.

Another creak, loud enough to wake him.

The wide circle of drool under his face was cold and slimy. His heart was back up in his neck, and his head pounded in time with every beat.

The pressure from lying on his bladder was an immediate signal of panic.

Then he heard the creak again. From the stairs leading up to his loft. The memory of the sedan at the edge of the field made him curl his lips in disgust. He *knew* they might come, and he still knocked the bottom out of a tequila bottle?

He stayed still. Crawled his fingers across the floor like a spider. The moon was sending its cold glow through the windows. A nice October sky. He could see his hand clearly against the oak planking.

Up to the nightstand where he eased the drawer open. Wrapped his fingers around the big stainless steel flashlight he kept in there. All metal construction and three big "D" batteries.

He pulled it out. Made a snorting grunt. Breathed as loudly as he could.

Another creak.

He couldn't tell where they were on the stairs. Halfway? Two from the top?

Then whoever was in the lead hit the bottle. Must have planted his foot right down on top of it. The glass rolled out from under him, and the floor shuddered from the impact of his fall. It must have knocked the breath right out of him.

Frank heard a sound from the floor. Something like, *Huuuuuuunn.*

A second voice cursed as feet hit the stairs in a rush.

Frank dropped his right leg to the floor. Dug his toes in and drew a deep breath.

Then he spun up from the bed with a roar. Let the

flashlight fly out from his outstretched fingers to where he guessed the man would be when he hit the landing up top.

The sound of the flashlight hitting the intruder in the chest was like a hundred-mile-an-hour strike landing in a catcher's mitt. A beautiful impact of dumb drunk luck.

Frank continued his spin off the other side of the bed. Down to the floor where he curled up in tight agony. The pull in his side felt like a knife ripping through.

The second guy was a staggering shadow. Feet tripped up on his fallen comrade. One arm wheeling out for balance. The other holding his chest like he was having a massive heart attack.

Frank worked onto his knees as the guy found his feet and bent over in pain. Frank hoped he had broken the guy's sternum.

Frank forced himself to his feet. He had no weapons. No defense against the gun in this guy's hand. Frank saw teeth flash in a pained grin. The glitter of reflected moonlight off the barrel.

He had only a railing behind the shooter, and the memory of sprinting up bleachers until he needed to puke.

He pushed off to cover the short distance with as much force as he could drive through his hips. Dropped down just before contact, and hit the guy with his shoulder sinking into his gut, right under his ribs.

Frank closed his eyes for what was coming, but instead of them both breaking through the railing and flying into the air — he even hoped they came down on top of the van — the railing cracked and rocked back, but held.

The guy folded back with a choked cry. His gun sailed from his hand.

Frank felt his neck whip back, and he stumbled back over the first guy's still-struggling body. The back of his head bounced off the floor, and the room bloomed into a burning white light.

His arms and legs moved. Flailing out for purchase, and he rolled over and onto his knees as his vision cleared. The second guy was on his knees. One arm over the sagging railing. The other one held against his chest. His face was a twisted grimace of pain.

The guy that had slipped on the tequila bottle made it to his feet, but he was stooped over, panting in tiny sips of air.

Frank figured this time might be the one, and he pushed to his feet for a second charge. Not nearly as impressive as the first one had been. Just knocking the first guy back into the second guy where they both clung to the railing for balance.

Frank fell back on his ass, teeth clacking together as he landed.

Right when the railing finally gave way.

They went over the edge and fell to the concrete below. This time, Frank hoped they *missed* the van. The wet snapping of their landing sounded like reassurance.

He managed to get to his feet. Made it over to the stairs without tripping on the tequila bottle. All the way to the bottom. The loft had been a traditional place to store hay in its prior life. Almost twenty feet up. It was a lot of stairs.

He bent over to catch his breath. Ventured out to see how they had done.

Not well.

The light was poor, but Frank was sure the guy on the bottom was dead. A splatter of blood had sprayed out from where his face had made contact with the ground.

The guy on top had fared better. Rolling side to side

and groaning, but there was blood in his teeth, and both arms seemed to bend in odd directions.

Frank walked over and dropped down. Dug into the guy's pockets until he found some keys. He leaned on him, and the guy curled up with a cry of pain.

"Are these to your car?" Frank asked.

The guy squeezed his eyes shut and nodded.

"Very good," Frank said.

The guy cried out again when Frank pushed off against his chest. Walked in a circle around them until he found both pistols. Then dropped back down with a growl of frustration so he could check for anything else.

One phone. A butterfly knife. No I.D.

Frank went to the back door. Squinted out into the night. Saw the moon glint off the car at the end of the driveway. Not too far.

He shuffled into the open. Kept his head down until he got to the car. Dropped in and gunned the engine. A Chrysler of some kind. He didn't really care.

He pulled it up to the door. Looked around for the trunk release for what felt like an hour before finding it.

Back to the guys who were still in their crumpled pile. The top guy still moaning. Frank shook his head in disgust. "Suck it up, Nancy."

He got the guy by the ankle and started dragging, sweating and out of breath by the time he arrived at the car. Hunched over his side.

Ain't nothing to it but to do it.

He got the guy into the trunk. Made more difficult by his struggles, and the whimpers of pain in his ear. He expected Mo to come running out at any moment, but maybe it wasn't as loud as Frank thought.

Back to the other guy, and as expected, it was easier

flopping the dead one up into the trunk. He wasn't struggling.

Frank slammed the lid. Got back behind the wheel and drove to the end of the lane. There was a county building a mile or so to the west. Bordered by a lot of overgrowth. Easy to put it there. Or maybe the old electric station to the east. Gravel piles and old shipping containers.

The station was closer, so Frank turned left.

When he got there, the gate was locked with a chain, but Frank put the nose of the sedan right up on it. Eased the car into it, the engine whining. Then it gave way with a snap that whipped his head again. Shooting fingers of ice down his spine.

He pulled the car toward the back where branches hung low to touch a dome of gravel. Past a row of rusting cubes that could make an excellent homeless shelter.

He got out. Tossed the phone into the gravel. Gave it a couple stomps, but his heart wasn't in it. His side screamed in protest whenever he lifted his boot.

There was a slight thump from the trunk. A muffled voice. Frank left it behind him as he staggered back to the gate.

He pulled it closed. Looped the chain back up so it looked like it was still holding. Turned around and dropped his head to take a few deep breaths. The abandoned power station had been closer, but he still had to walk all the way back.

Chapter Twenty-Five

THE PAIN WOKE him a little before Mo's shouting voice.

"What the *fuck*?"

It took Frank two tries before he could finally sit up. When he made it to his feet, he couldn't stand straight up. Bent over like an old man.

He walked over to the stairs without picking his feet up.

At the top, he looked down to see Mo standing at the bloodstain in the middle of a scatter of railing debris.

He held his hands out to his sides. Looked up at Frank. Pointed to the blood. Then he pointed to the trail leading out the back door.

Frank shook his head. Dismissed the question with a flap of his hand before turning around to make his way to the coffeemaker. One of those off-brand pod types that brewed in seconds instead of his drip machine.

It tasted like garbage, but it was fast. He didn't need *good*, he just needed something *now*.

Mo must have taken his time, because he just got to the top of the stairs as Frank was taking his first sip. He sighed in pleasure. Not at the taste, but the heat. The *experience*.

"Frank … buddy. What is going on?"

Frank smiled over his cup. "You tell me. I just woke up."

Mo pointed at Frank's chest. "You look like dogshit. Is that your blood?"

Frank shook his head. Told the story of the two unfortunate souls that snuck up on him in the night. Then he looked around Mo's side. Saw that the bottle had almost rolled back beneath the bed.

Mo watched without comment as Frank bent gingerly down to retrieve it. Then he carried the bottle into the kitchen and returned it to the shelf.

"And there it'll stay." He stood and met Mo's gaze. "You know, for luck."

Mo held one hand up in dismissal. Shook his head in disbelief. Walked to the stairs without saying a word. Paused to look over the edge. Shook his head again as he descended. Walked out into the morning sun.

Frank stepped out onto the balcony with his coffee. Shielded his eyes as Mo made it across the yard to the RV. There were bags stacked against the front wheel. He was still shaking his head when he opened the side door to put them inside.

Frank finished his coffee, almost burning his tongue. Then he took a long, cold shower. There was still tenderness everywhere, but it was tolerable as he dried off and got dressed. He finished with a holster clipped to the back of his waistband. The butterfly knife he had gotten from Thing 1 … or had it been Thing 2?

He dropped it in his pocket. Slid into his flip-flops before grabbing a couple bottles and heading to the house.

Gen stopped him before he made it to the porch. She pulled him into the shade of the big oak out front.

"We need to go over how to take care of him, okay?"
Her eyes were red.

Frank smiled, but shook his head. "I don't think so."

"But Frank, if you don't—"

"Gen." He put the bottles under one arm to hold her hands. "I know how to take care of him."

Her face crumpled into grief, and she lunged forward to wrap him in a shaking embrace. He gritted his teeth against the pain her strong arms caused. Stood there and took it until she was ready to step back.

She put one hand on his cheek. Smiled through her tears. "He is such a good soul. The world will be different without a man like him in it."

"I know."

She nodded. "Or a man like you."

She whirled away and marched to the RV. The door slammed behind her.

Frank turned to the porch, and saw Mo with his giant arms crossed over his broad chest.

"My man!" Mo shouted.

Frank nodded as he walked to the porch. Put one of the bottles on the railing. A rye bourbon he had gotten at some liquor store or another. The second bottle was a Tres Amigos tequila. One of his favorites. He uncorked it. Took a drink off the top. Handed the bottle up to Mo.

He took it. "I don't touch this stuff no more." Then a pull for himself, swallowed with a wince before he handed the bottle back. "I'll see you."

Frank didn't voice his doubt.

They passed each other on the steps, and Frank turned to watch him walk away. Waited until he heard the RV. Watched them turn into the road and turn out of sight at the stop sign.

He took his bottles inside. Set them on the island before cutting into GG's room. Stopped just inside the door to find the wheelchair sitting next to the bed. One of GG's legs dangling off the side. "Help me in there, Dad."

Through some trial and error, and a lot of cursing from GG, they got him situated without breaking anything. Both of them breathless and pale. Frank sweating despite how cool it was in the house.

GG leaned back as his pump bubbled away. "When they coming back?"

Frank sat on the edge of the bed. "They didn't say, but it'll probably only be a couple of days. Through the end of the week. Until we get our business taken care of."

GG grinned. "The business of killing me?"

"At least." Frank nodded, pointing to GG's bare legs. "You want a blanket?"

"Fuck no. I can't feel 'em anyway."

Frank pointed at his head. "What about one of those beanie things?"

GG rolled his eye. "Gen is the absolutest, that's for sure, but that thing just makes me hot and itchy."

He tipped his head at the stand carrying his morphine pump. "I got that thing jacked up. Let's get out to the porch. I wanna listen to the rain."

Frank glanced at the sun shining against the backs of the curtain. Shrugged as he got behind the chair and threaded through the door. He paused at the island for the bottles. Snapped his fingers when he realized he needed a glass. Went around to get one, but froze in front of the sink.

"It's the one next to the fridge," GG said. "Get one for me too."

His words were slurred form his numb side. From so

much narcotics. Add alcohol to the mix, and Frank didn't think the conversation would last very long.

The temperature had dropped quite a bit since being inside. A dark line of clouds in the southern sky. Looked like GG was going to get his rain after all.

Frank wheeled the chair in front of the window. Stepped on the rubber brake. Sat in the white rocker next to the little table. Poured two glasses. Leaned over with a wheezing grunt to hand the second glass into GG's good hand.

Rain started to patter on the grass as he raised a toast. "To you, buddy."

GG closed his eyes. "Why me?"

"Because I can't think of anything better."

GG burst into laughter that ended in a coughing fit. He held his glass away from his body until it passed. Lifted his glass to join Frank's. Knocked it back like water.

When he held his glass over for more, Frank didn't hesitate.

GG set himself upright, and closed his eyes. "Will it hurt?"

Frank took a sip. "Will *what* hurt?"

"The end."

Frank thought about what his daughter went through at *her* end. Then he shook his head. "Probably not as much as the life before it did."

GG knocked his second drink back. A small shudder as it went down. He blew his breath out as if blowing on a hot bite of pizza. "I'm fucking scared, Dad."

"About what?"

Tears from his good eye as he held his glass out for another. "I'm afraid I won't know anybody when I get to heaven. Or even worse, I'm afraid they won't know me. Like I'll see *you* up there, and you'll look right through me."

Frank poured liquid into the shaking glass. Filled his own up before answering. He knew the *you* GG was talking about was his *real* father, and not the stand-in he'd found in Frank.

"Of course you'll know everybody. And they'll know you. And even if they don't, as soon as they meet you, they'll love you."

"How do you know?" GG asked.

Frank leaned over and grabbed his shoulder. "Because I love you, buddy."

GG drank his third shot, and tequila dribbled out of the numb side of his mouth. He shook his head like somebody trying to get water out of his face. "Thanks, Dad."

A cool gust blew across the porch. Crisp with the rain it carried. GG smiled. Swayed back and forth like a tree out in the open. "Can you get me my pillow, Dad. I think I'm gonna wanna sleep here tonight. Would that be okay?"

Frank smiled. "Absolutest."

He patted GG's head on his way by, and when he got inside, he leaned back against the door and cried into his hands. Biting into his palm to keep from making any noise. He didn't want GG to hear.

He wiped his eyes. Made it into GG's room where he grabbed the top pillow from his bed. A grinning narwhal jumping over a rainbow.

When he got back outside, GG's head was hanging to the side. Drool had already made a small wet circle on his shoulder.

Frank wedged the pillow behind GG's shoulders. Eased his head back into it. Put his hands in his lap. Got back in his own chair to drink some more. Listen to the rain.

He tipped his head back like GG. Laced his fingers over his belly. Closed his eyes.

THE SOUND of shattering glass made Frank sit forward in his chair with a gasp.

He looked around in confusion, unable to penetrate the darkness.

He heard crickets instead of the rain. Then another crash. Distant. Like it was coming from the back yard.

GG snorted. Smacked his lips. Rolled into a gentle snore.

Frank stood and staggered to the top of the stairs. Felt for the first step with his toe. Dropped down on it to repeat the process twice more before he felt mulch underfoot.

His side hurt. Kidneys ached. Head pounded over his sore neck. What a mess.

He leaned against the big oak and fumbled with his zipper. Finally got into position to pee without dripping onto his feet.

Heard another smash from the back yard. It sounded like it was all the way in the back. Maybe the barn.

Clouds were covering the moon, and the darkness was like a blanket hanging in front of his face.

He made it to the shed, where he paused to rest with his forehead against the rough wood. Then he leaned past the edge to see flashlight beams flickering around the barn. Through the open doors and from the upstairs windows.

From the sounds of the breaking glass, somebody inside was angry. Maybe at not finding what they thought was going to be there.

He stood in the dark. Waiting to see what happened. Wondering if he would have to draw his gun for a confrontation. Go back to the porch to protect GG?

He reached behind him. Paused when the lights went out. Moments later he heard an engine start. Almost indistinguishable from the rush of sound caused by wind and bugs.

Frank stood next to the shed for several minutes, before finally giving up like the flashlights had. Made his way back to the porch to sit back down.

Back into his earlier position.

Chapter Twenty-Six

THE SUN SEEMED to be shining directly into Frank's open mouth. Baking the saliva into a salty scum.

He leaned forward, but hissed in pain as his neck straightened.

"Hurts, don't it?" GG whispered.

Frank cracked his right eye open. Looked over to see GG sitting with his head hanging forward. The good half of his mouth in a smile.

Frank sighed. Rubbed his eyes. "We're not dead?"

GG shook his head. "Only feels like it."

His pump bubbled. Frank wondered how much morphine could be in the thing. He told GG what happened last night. "But I can't be sure until I get back there and check."

"Can you get me back inside, Dad? I'm pretty tired."

"Of course, buddy," Frank said, but he didn't get up immediately. He struggled to his feet and stretched. Took several breaths. Until he could finally move without shooting pain in his side, or his heart pounding up into his jaw.

He wheeled GG over to the door. Pulled him backward into a wave of refreshing AC. Got him all the way into his room without running into any furniture or walls. Paused next to the bed. "I'm not sure how we're gonna handle this, buddy."

"Just get me up there."

Frank pointed at GG's lap. "What about … do we need to change you?"

GG shook his head. Hissed in pain at the movement. "Ain't nothing in it but a little bit of wee. Just get me in bed, Dad. Lemme have this."

"Have what?"

GG looked up with a smile. "Everything that's been happening to me hasn't been my fault. Just fucking wasting away as this thing eats me from the inside out. But this hangover …" He closed his eyes. Took a few breaths before continuing. "It's *my* fault."

Frank understood. Not the need to suffer, but the need to make himself suffer. Like the pain he was about to put himself through getting GG in bed.

Much like the day before, they were both gray-faced and hurting by the time they were done. Frank asked if GG needed anything, but a snore was his only answer. Frank went into the kitchen to fill a glass with water from the fridge dispenser. Drank it down and filled the glass again.

Some caretaker he was.

He could barely take care of himself.

He went out the side door. Looked down at the ground to keep as much sun out of his eyes as he could. Almost ran into the barn next to the open door.

The van seemed okay. Apparently they hadn't vented their frustration on it. That was something, because when Frank got upstairs, that was something *else*.

He saw what he expected. Drawers pulled out and emptied. Mattress turned over. Broken glass littering the floor. He thought about sliding his flip-flops off and stomping through it, but that was a bit much.

Frank found his phone on the floor next to a puddle made from the water in a vase shaped like a margarita glass. The flowers had been long dead. No big loss.

The phone needed a charge, but the charging pad was down on the workbench. He gritted his teeth and made the journey. It felt like he had sprinted a mile by the time he got back upstairs.

He tried to puzzle out what was happening while he showered. Waiting for the door to burst open. A gun pushed through the curtain.

What had they wanted? Surely just to kill him in his sleep like the last two. Or maybe to discover what had happened to them.

Had they seen the RV pull away? Now that they had found the barn empty, would they come back, or did they think Frank left too?

Had Wilson told the truth about Jennifer and Becka?

He found some clothes that hadn't been stepped on in the dark. Didn't bother with a comb, just pushing hair back with his fingers.

He ate an oatmeal cream pie with a cup of garbage coffee. Took his time on the stairs. Finally got to the phone and powered it back on. One notification from ten last night.

A single text: *Call me bitch*.

Frank left his cup on the bench. Walked outside to stand with his face turned up to the sun. Sucked in a deep breath before continuing on to Carmen's grave.

He pulled the phone up, and instead of the number Stan was texting from, he dialed another. One he didn't even need to get out of his journal. Because Frank had dreamed of dialing this number a thousand times.

He hadn't considered the day or the time. Or whether she would answer.

"Hello?" Her voice sounded sleepy. Like the call had pulled her out of a deep sleep.

"Freya? Is This Freya Dahl?"

The silence was like waiting for the bandage to pull away from a scab.

"Mr. Grimm? *Frank?*"

"Yes, it's me. How have you been?"

"How have I been? I thought you were dead!"

"I'm so sorry."

"The cops came. Asked me and my mom all about you. Then the *media* started coming around again. It was Heirloom all over!"

This was a bad idea. Frank pulled the phone away. Brought it back up. Missed the last thing she said.

Frank ran his thumb over the button to end their call, but unable to afford the cowardice, he returned the phone to his ear. "Sorry. I didn't hear you."

"Stop apologizing!"

Frank swallowed the *I'm sorry* on his lips. "Okay."

She sighed. "I asked what happened."

He told her. A little bit of it. Not because Frank wanted Freya to know, but because he still needed to hear her voice. She was one he had saved. Because of him, she had a life better than the one full of abuse she had been living. Because of him, she now had a choice.

Where none of the other girls did.

She settled into his story.

He paused at the sound of her quietly crying. "Please, don't cry."

"But you've been through so much, and I feel so bad for yelling at you."

"No, no. I should have called. Told you what was going on. I'm just … Freya, I'm so lost. And I miss you. And I miss Jenny." He broke into a sob. "And I want so much for you, baby. I want so much …"

Frank was overtaken by his tears. Crying into the phone while a little girl tried to comfort him from so very far away.

He heard the muffled sound of Irene's voice in the background.

"It's my mom," Freya told him. "I have to get ready for school."

Frank sniffed. Wiped his eyes. "Isn't it late?"

"Not here. We're like an hour behind you guys."

He grunted. Some detective.

"I'm sorry," she said, "but I have to go."

"Stop apologizing."

She giggled, and it sounded like dew dripping on rose petals.

"Call me this weekend? Please?"

"Of course," he said.

"Any time, okay?"

"I promise."

Another pause where the silence was the precipice of a fall. "I love you."

"I love you too, baby."

The phone went dead, and his hand fell. He looked away from the mound of Carmen's grave before raising it again, this time to dial Stan.

The click of the connection opening, then, "It's about fucking time."

"Hey," Frank said.

NOLON KING & DAIVD W. WRIG…

"What are you doing?" Stan asked.

"Nothing."

"Perfect."

Frank rocked from foot to foot. "What about you?"

"Nothing."

"Perfect."

Stan snorted laughter. "Look, I been watching you. It seems like you're fucking shit up worse than usual."

"Actually, for once, I think I'm doing okay."

"How do you figure?"

Frank sighed through his nose. "I made a plan, and now I'm executing it."

"Successfully?"

"Mostly."

Stan sucked air through his teeth. "You gonna make it out?"

"I really don't know."

"You want me to come in heavy?"

Frank wanted to see his cousin. Ached for the family he missed so much, but he shook his head anyway. "I don't think so."

So much time passed that Frank thought he may have lost the call.

"You know," Stan finally said. "One of these days you'll see what you're worth. Maybe you'll even forgive yourself. And you'll see that I'm right."

"About what?"

"About how much you mattered, man. About how much you were loved."

"I don't know," Frank said.

"That's your problem. You never did. I'm going back home, so call me this weekend."

"Okay."

And then he was gone too. The only one left was waiting in his room for Frank to come in and kill him with a morphine overdose. He looked up at the cloudless sky.

Why not? It seemed like a good day for it.

Chapter Twenty-Seven

FRANK WENT INSIDE and put his phone back on the charger. Dug through his ruined loft to find the cooler. Filled it with ice from the freezer. Then threw in everything he could think of that a couple of bros would want while celebrating.

It was GG's last day on earth. If Frank was lucky, it would be his too.

They would be back for him tonight, and this time they would check the house. Especially when all the lights were on. Like a beacon.

Frank lugged the cooler all the way to the house. Into the front door where he made plenty of noise. He dropped it at the foot of GG's bed.

His eyes fluttered open. "Hey, Dad."

Frank slid into the seat. "Hey, buddy. What do you wanna do today?"

"Nothing." GG shrugged. "I'm kinda thirsty, though."

His breath sounded like it was passing through pudding. Wet and thick. The deep hollows under his eyes were almost entirely black.

Frank dug in the cooler. Found a blue Gatorade. "First, let's get those electrolytes up."

He opened the bottle, and leaned over to grab GG's straw from the other table. Grunting at the end of his reach.

When he got it he held it up to GG's mouth and watched as nearly half of it went down.

GG leaned back with a sigh. "That was good. I was pretty thirsty."

Frank pulled out a cold bottle of beer up for himself.

"I ain't scared anymore," GG said. "But can we wait? Just a little while?"

"Of course."

GG fumbled around for his remote. Finally found it in a fold of the sheets. Clicked the TV on, and the screen filled with a cartoon. Frank had never seen it, but he watched. Laughed along with GG, paying closer attention whenever he pointed.

Every time he looked at his watch, Frank was shocked by how much time had passed. It would happen tonight. After GG was tired enough to finally fall asleep.

Frank would do it then.

But night was coming faster than he wanted.

And what if they came for Frank while he was pressing the button?

So be it.

He had heard Freya's voice. A little bit of her new independence and spirit. She had sounded so different already. Fierce. Beautiful. *Alive*.

Like GG had been.

Frank excused himself with the lie that he needed to use the bathroom, hating the thought of GG seeing him weep.

He reached into his cooler on the way by. Pulled out a

fresh beer from his stock that was dwindling too quickly. Tapped his glass rim against the plastic Gatorade bottle in a silent toast. Knocked the beer back in one long series of gulps.

"Can we wait until dark?" GG asked.

"Of course, buddy." Frank looked out the window at the dimming sky. It wouldn't be long now.

Then he remembered the second bottle sitting out on the island. Only two drinks missing.

He patted GG's knee on the way by. Came back with the bottle and a pair of glasses.

GG chuckled. It sounded like rustling paper. "One more for the road, huh Dad?"

"That's right."

This time the shot had GG coughing until he gagged. Bent over the side of his bed in case he threw up. Leaned back with his mouth hanging open to catch his breath.

Frank got ready to go get the paperclip. Reached down to take GG's curled hand in his. "I think it's about time, buddy."

"Wait," GG gasped. "I ain't ready."

"Are you scared again?"

"No, I just ain't ready. I need to be ready."

"How?"

GG closed his eyes. "Can you hold my hand, Dad?"

"I *am* holding your hand, buddy."

"That's good."

He settled, and his breath slowed. Deepened as he neared sleep.

"I'll remember you," GG whispered.

Frank put a hand against his forehead and cried until GG was fully asleep.

Then he filled his glass.

～

FRANK WASN'T sure what woke him up this time. A change in the air? A noise?

GG breathed in a wheezing rasp. Steady and unlabored. A clock ticked outside the room. Crickets and frogs in the yard.

The sound from GG's cartoon was so low it was barely at the level of hearing. Maybe that? Some weird sound effect?

But then Frank felt it again. A disturbance in the air over his head. Like somebody was standing over him.

"I know you're awake, old man." The voice was soft. Almost apologetic. "Sit up straight."

Frank did as he was asked, and the room came out from under him. He clamped down on the rising bile in his throat. Tipped his head back with a groan.

"Jesus," said another voice. "You drink that whole bottle by yourself?"

The first voice snickered. "You give any to Cancer Jim here? He looks like he passed out *hours* ago."

"And *smells* like he pissed himself."

Frank smiled. Nodded his head as if agreeing with every word. He wanted to puke in their faces. Stomp on them when they fell to the floor in disgust.

If he could just make the room stop spinning.

"Now get up, Grimm," ordered the first voice.

Frank opened his eyes, and by the light of the TV screen saw who was talking to him. "I know you, right?"

"The fuck should I know if you know me or not?"

It was one of Owens' men from Playa Dolor. The one that went back to wait in the car. Must have been the one that helped Owens after Stan stabbed him in the neck.

Frank nodded. "You should have put the tourniquet on Owens a little tighter."

The guy laughed. "You're not the only one that thinks so. Come *on*."

Frank tried to pretend he was drunk, but there was little to his ruse. He *was* drunk. Stupid, selfish old man.

The other guy leaned over GG's bed. "The fuck is wrong with this zombie head, anyway?"

GG's hand shot up from his side. Clamped on the guy's throat. The tendons stood out under his wrist.

Frank's guy threw himself back with a shout while GG's guy brought his gun down on the invalid's forearm.

Frank remembered the shocking strength in those fingers. Knew the guy had no chance.

Frank's guy brought his pistol around, and Frank jumped up from his chair with a cracking bellow. Hit the guy spread out to drive him back into the TV.

It tumbled back behind the dresser, and the sound of the plastic crashing to the floor was drowned out by the pistol firing into Frank's hip.

Burning pain down his leg. Choking sounds behind him.

He had the guy's wrist in both hands. Pushed the gun away from his body. A fist looped up into Frank's face. Cracked off his scarred eyebrow. He felt it split open. Blood poured in to obscure his vision.

He kept his grip, but lifted his feet. Pulling on the guy's arm with all his weight, then turning into the guy's body to land on his elbow.

The bone snapped, and the guy's arm folded under him as they landed.

The scream in Frank's ear was a spike through his brain.

He let go of the guy's useless wrist. Rolled up onto his

head to drive both elbows down into his face. Until the blood flew up into the air, and the guy went limp.

Frank threw himself to the side, reaching for the guy's gun.

Then he remembered the one at the small of his back. He reached behind him, but the room filled with another two cracks. The echoes were followed by a buzzing whine that drowned out every other noise.

Frank drew his gun and spun to face the bed.

The other guy was practically hanging from GG's grip, his face bloated and red. Eyes bugging. Pistol dangling from his loose fingers.

Two ragged holes spread red across GG's stomach. His teeth were bared. Good eye intent on his victim. With a scream of rage, he jerked his hand back, tearing the guy's throat out to spatter his face with flesh and blood.

He sat back with a satisfied smile. Looked at Frank as his eyelids fluttered closed. "I don't feel anything at all."

Frank reeled back in horror. His sweet friend was dead, but he had no time to mourn. Footsteps pounding through the house. A loud question that sounded like it was shouted through a bale of wool. "You good, Holmes?"

Frank didn't know which one was Holmes. The one drowning in his own blood, or the one waking up from a savage beating.

Didn't matter. They were both about to be dead. Frank dropped down in front of the guy he wrestled.

"Talk to me, Holmes!" From somewhere … maybe near the living room?

Frank put his gun against the guy's temple and pulled the trigger twice.

Pushed himself to his feet as the guy sagged to the floor. Limped to put himself behind the door. Watched through a crack between the hinges.

"Motherfucker!" A hissed whisper.

Blood dripped down Frank's leg. Along the outside of his foot to soak his flip-flop.

The tip of a shotgun peeked through the doorway. A dark hand on the stock. A finger quivering on the trigger. The gunman's panting breath coming in short gasps.

"What's in there?" asked a voice from the kitchen.

The gunman only shook his head as he crept inside.

He disappeared from the crack, only to reappear on the other side of the door as he entered.

Frank threw himself against the door with a bellow of effort.

The gunman's shotgun roared as the door made contact.

Frank drove it with his shoulder to shove his enemy into GG's nightstand. Bending over to smash the lamp, moving his hand from the stock and planting it on GG's bed to keep from sliding to the floor.

Frank slipped in his own blood and fell against the gunman's side. Grabbed a handful of his jacket to stay on him and shoved the gun up under his chin.

Fired twice. Flinched away from the spray.

As Frank pulled the shotgun from his loosening fingers, the guy in the kitchen let loose.

He also liked shotguns.

The blast blew a half moon out of the door, and a burning chunk out of Frank's shoulder. Sprayed him with wood shrapnel and steel shot.

The side of his face and neck burned as Frank landed hard on his back. Rolled half under the bed while racking another shell into the breach, only to be stopped when the gunman's dead body flopped on top of him, pinning Frank to the metal rail and his shotgun to the floor.

The guy from the kitchen filled the doorway, shotgun

sweeping back and forth in front of him. Frank could see him through a gap under the dead gunman's still-dripping chin.

The new guy stepped in to put his foot right in front of Frank's barrel.

He squeezed the trigger and his shot blew most of the guy's ankle into burger.

The recoil tore the shotgun from Frank's hand. The new guy's leg folded, and he screamed, firing into the ceiling as he fell.

Frank struggled out from under the weight of the dead gunman. Sliding in his own blood. And someone else's. Leaking brains.

The new gunman brought his shotgun around, his eyes widening in panic and agony. Frank didn't bother knocking it aside. He hadn't cocked a new shell in yet.

He got to his knees. Slid his shotgun out. Racked in a shell and put the barrel against the side of the guy's neck.

He dropped his shotgun. Held both hands out to the side. His body shuddered with his sobs.

Frank spread the guy's neck into a fan across the floor.

Then he used the shotgun as a cane to help him stand. Let it fall from his hands as he became steady. Frank's pulse felt like somebody was punching him in the side of the neck. He couldn't draw a deep enough breath. Had trouble feeling his fingers.

He leaned over the dead guy against the bed to reach out and touch GG's face.

"I'll remember you," he said.

Chapter Twenty-Eight

FRANK WALKED through the house like he was already dead. His arms hanging at his side. Head swiveling back and forth, but not really seeing.

Nobody in any of the rooms. No voices. No nothing.

He made it all the way to the back bedroom. The master suite.

Looked out the back window to see light shining across the yard. The doors to the barn wide open. He had left them open, same as he usually did. But had he left the lights on?

Probably not. It was bright morning the last time he'd been there.

Maybe it was Owens out there.

He walked out of the bedroom to the side door. The RV would usually be parked right outside, but Mo and Gen were gone. He wondered where they were. They never said, and he didn't want to know in case somebody asked. Waterboarding or torture or however people got people to talk.

He was still curious. Hoped they were near the water.

On the last step, his hip gave out, throwing him into the yard where he barely caught himself before smashing his face on the ground.

He wanted to lie there and catch his breath. Maybe just rest for a bit. His breath was loud in the grass. Probably scaring off the bugs.

He pushed himself up. Cocked his head to listen. It was quiet. Crickets in the distance, but not nearby. Spooked at his bumbling human noise.

No sirens either. Had nobody heard the gunfire? Had Owens called the response off?

Assuming Owens was even here.

Frank wanted to find out, so he got back to his feet. Staggered toward the barn.

He looked up at the light, but could only see the bright shape of the open doorway. Blurry blobs of color inside. He squinted as he stepped through onto the concrete. Turned in a slow circle, but there was nobody there.

He looked down at his bloody footprints on the ground.

"We're up here, Frank."

He jerked his head toward the sound. Gasped at the pain shooting up his neck. Continued to look up until he saw Owens standing at the top of the stairs.

He seemed smaller. Not quite as broad. Arms slightly less thick. Getting stabbed in the neck probably wasn't good for gains. Otherwise, the man was in much better shape than Frank.

Owens shook his head. "I am surprised as absolute shit up here, Frank. We had something very special planned for you, but it looks like things have changed."

Frank swallowed. Nodded slowly. "Yeah. I killed them."

"Fucking amazing. Still … come on up. We don't have much time."

Then he heard it. The distant wail of a siren. But who was responding? Somebody Owens controlled? One of Wilson's men? Or somebody Frank could trust?

Frank waved him back. "Okay, I'm coming."

He headed to the stairs, barely getting his feet to drag over the debris left by the broken railing. Passing the bench, Frank pulled his phone off the charger. Dropped it in his pocket so he could call 911 later. Stopped in confusion when he remembered the sirens.

He shrugged to himself as he reached the stairs. Gritted his teeth in pain with every step. Leaning against the wall along with his ascent.

At the top, Frank turned to find Owens sitting on the edge of his bed. His gasping breath turned into a grieving wail at the sight of Jennifer sitting beside him.

Frank fell to his knees, and Owens looked at him with a wide grin.

"This was what we had planned. We were going to rape this sweet ... innocent little girl. Right in front of you. In *your* bed. They would have found you dead on top of her cooling body. Overdosed on heroin. Everybody would have been right about you."

Jennifer looked at Frank with the wide staring eyes he remembered from the upper floor. No emotion except for a curious waiting. An empty expectation.

He could see the bruising creeping up past the collar of her shirt. Down her arms. The raised welts that had wept blood.

The burns around her wrists where she had been tied up.

"Where's Becka?" Frank asked.

Owens grunted. "She's gone. Dead like *all* the girls you didn't save. But not before we had our fun."

Frank remembered her on the table. How much more *fun* could they have had?

His mind recoiled at the question, and he curled forward, unable to keep straight under the weight of his guilt.

The sirens were much closer. What would they see when they got here?

Frank sat back on his heels, realizing exactly what was happening here. Owens would kill Jennifer, then Frank. With the support of the monsters that had been propping him up this whole time, Owens would be a hero. And Frank would finally be framed for the rape and murder of the only girl that really meant anything to Owens. The one he had raped and murdered. The one he had failed to pin on Frank. The one that had almost led to an entire sex trafficking ring being destroyed, bringing his network of contacts and enslavers along with it.

Jenny Grimm.

The other girls Owens could pin on Frank were a bonus.

Owens put his arm around Jennifer's shoulders. Pulled her in toward him. When she resisted, he grabbed her throat and jerked her close, but his soft smile remained. "Too bad there's no time to have a little fun, though. I would tear this little bitch in half. Like what I did to your daughter, Frank. I'm telling you, she was exquisite."

Frank looked into her panicked eyes. Widening as she began to fight for air. A plea for help. A silent scream.

Frank heard his daughter's voice. Crying. Begging. Pleading for help. Shouting it for anybody to hear, but nobody came. She died wondering why her daddy didn't save her.

Frank drove his fists into his thighs. One dug in painfully. The other one was stopped by something in his pocket that tore into his knuckles. He pulled his hand away to see the blood streaming down his fingers. Looked up at Jennifer holding onto Owens' powerful forearm.

Frank stood and pulled the butterfly from his pocket. Took a step toward Owens as he opened it. No flourish. No whipping the knife into an artistic blur like in a movie. He just let it fall open. Wrapped his fingers around it. And claimed another step.

Owens opened his hand. Jennifer fell back with a coughing sob. Put her hands to her throat and turned to cough violently into the comforter.

"Stay back!" Owens shouted.

Frank remembered the bleachers. Heard GG's shout of encouragement. Rose up onto his toes and pushed into a sprint.

"Hey!" Owens shouted again, this time reaching into his jacket.

Frank held the knife in front of him. Opened his mouth in a scream.

Owens drew a revolver from his shoulder holster. Rose from the bed into a crouch. Aimed and fired, too late.

Heat blossomed across Frank's chest as the knife entered Owens' left eye. Searing pain that silenced his scream as another shot rang out.

The blade went through muscle and bone. Deep into the skull. Frank crashed into Owens' outstretched hand. Carried through into his body, and they fell back onto the floor in a heap.

Was he hearing sirens or screams? It didn't matter. Frank struggled up onto all fours so he could look down at Owens' face. Slack with death. Half covered in blood.

His vision dimmed. He shook his head, and blood trickled from his mouth. It felt like he was trying to pull air through a stack of pillows.

He managed to stand, only to fall backward onto the bed, hands lifeless between his knees, and toes pointed in opposite directions.

The sirens were *very* loud now.

As the bed rocked under Jennifer's weight, Frank smiled. He had reached down inside himself. Found something of worth. A virtue he had hidden even from himself … and Jenny was alive. He turned to look at her face. The sweet face he remembered.

Frank smiled, taking her into his arms. Soothed her by rubbing her back like he used to do. Cried as he took in a sip of air that smelled like her hair.

He needed to tell Stan about this moment. Shifted Jenny's weight to his other thigh so he could get his phone out. Struggled to see as he typed in his message. The screen kept blurring.

Finally satisfied, Frank sent the message, then threw the phone out into the air where it fell out of sight and shattered on the concrete below.

He held Jenny against his chest. Realized he could no longer hear the sirens. Only his heartbeat, bursting with joy.

Then soon, that too faded.

Chapter Twenty-Nine

STAN BENT over his knee to inspect the scar over the stump halfway down his shin. Red and twisted, it was soft and pliable. Painless as he ran his fingers over it. Healing nicely.

Music from the kitchen made him smile. Earth, Wind & Fire. Very tasty. It was Ronnie's favorite, and she would usually be dancing whenever it was on.

He leaned back so he could see through the doorway, and he wasn't disappointed.

She wore an apron and nothing else, and his vantage point from the edge of the bed let him see everything that was shaking to the music. Dark brown skin glistening with sweat. Hair pulled back in a tight bun. She danced with abandon in front of the stove. A potholder in one hand. A wooden spoon in the other. The aroma was almost as enticing as the view.

She had made sure he stayed in bed. *Active recovery* she called it. And lots of nutrition. They had known each other for a long time, and she was familiar with his appetites. They'd had plenty of hard years together. Both of them needing the kind of help that the other wasn't capable of providing.

Stan couldn't forgive himself, and she couldn't love herself.

For him, it was his failure in Afghanistan. For her, it was the mask of scar tissue that made her face look like a streaked pumpkin.

She couldn't believe that anybody could find her beautiful. But he could. Because she *was*.

Stan had to look away before her sensuous hips stirred something up. They'd been in bed for hours. Making sure he got his prescribed amount of exercise. Midnight had found them ready for a break, and Ronnie suggested pasta. She knew he loved the carbs. Eating it by the pot. And he had lost so much weight fighting the infection from the alligator's bite. Dealing with the pain of the surgery. All the rehab.

Thank God for *her*. How lucky was he that she had taken him back so readily? That she herself had thought she was the lucky one?

He slipped the sock over his stump. Fitted the prosthetic leg over it. Pumped down until it seated. Leaned back to extend both legs. The weight was so even, Stan could barely tell them apart. If he focused, he could almost feel the missing toes wiggle.

The replacement foot was a mechanical lump of flexible plastic and aluminum. Lots of little screws and adjustments he could tweak — though most felt useless. Or like placebos. The crosswalk button that didn't actually change the timing of the traffic lights.

Standing was much like it had been. A simple matter of where he put his weight. Anatomical leverage and a build-up of new muscles. Stan needed all the practice he could get. Frank had opened up a mess, and he was keen on opening it even wider.

Ronnie had agreed. While they were lying next to each other. As he was tracing tiny circles around her nipple, she had told him that he was going to do it, and that was that.

He would find evil men that were preying on women, and if he couldn't bring them to justice, he would kill them. He had so much to pay for, and only his own life to give. Maybe he could augment that fee with the souls of others.

Sweeten the pot.

Stan got to his feet. Just a pinching pressure, but no pain. He was getting so close to full recovery. Better than ever.

He glanced into the kitchen. Almost got mesmerized by watching her hips again when he heard his phone vibrate from the corner table. He walked over to get it, wanting to ask her how long it was going to be. He wasn't really hungry. He just needed to eat. That old compulsion to fill his belly.

Stan picked up his phone and unlocked it with his thumbprint. Swiped the notifications down to see a text from Frank, smiling as he opened it.

You were right.

The phone blurred through his tears. He pressed it to his forehead and cried. Heaving sobs that left him trembling. He took deep breaths. Felt the rhythm in his mind. Brought it into his center where he focused on linking his imagination with reality. Making his body calm and healthy.

Easing his anxiety away.

The panic subsided. Then it was replaced with joy. If the text was real, Frank had won. He had found beauty in himself. Just like Stan knew he would.

He walked into the kitchen. Cozied up to Ronnie as she dropped into another rocking step of her dance. She moaned in pleasure. Turned to look into his face. Drew back in concern at the sight of his tears. "Baby, what's wrong?"

Her emotions didn't show through the scars, but Stan knew her. Saw the worry in the lines around her eyes. The tightening of the stripes of skin on her cheeks. He bent to kiss her. Felt the ridge of the grafts around her lips. The shrunken cartilage of her nose.

He pulled her against him. Poured his passion into her, finally pulling back so they could each catch their breath. He smiled at her confusion. "Nothing at all," he whispered.

She tilted her head. "I don't know if I believe you."

He shrugged. "It's true, though."

She pointed to the noodles simmering in meat sauce. "Then are you ready to eat? It's done."

Stan shook his head. "I don't think so."

She dropped the spoon with a gasp of shock.

He took her face between his hands. "I think I'm finally full."

Corrupt men in the justice system ruined his cousin, Frank Grimm, now Stan Manning is going to make them pay. Starting with Senator Royse Mickelson.

Read Cold Justice today!

A Quick Favor

Thanks for reading *Hidden Virtue*.

If you enjoyed this book, please consider writing a review of it on your favorite bookselling site so other readers can enjoy it too. Just a couple of sentences would mean a lot to me.

Thank you!

Nolon & Dave

About the Authors

Nolon King writes fast-paced psychological thrillers set in the glitzy world of entertainment's power players with a bold, insightful voice. He's not afraid to explore the darker side of human nature through stories featuring families torn apart by secrets and lies.

Nolon loves to write about big questions and moral quandaries. How far would you go to cover up an honest mistake? Would you destroy your career to protect your family? How much of your soul would you sell to get the life of your dreams? Would you cheat on your husband to keep your children safe? Would you give in to a stalker's demands to save your marriage?

David W. Wright is the co-author of edge-of-your-seat thrillers including the best-selling post-apocalyptic series *Yesterday's Gone,* the paranoid sci-fi *WhiteSpace* series, and the vigilante series, *No Justice,* as well as standalone thrillers *12,* and *Crash* which was recently optioned for a movie.

David is an accomplished, though intermittent, cartoonist who lives in [LOCATION REDACTED] with his wife and son [NAMES REDACTED.]

He is not at all paranoid.

He is "the grumpy one" on *The Story Studio Podcast* with fellow Sterling and Stone founders, Sean Platt and Johnny B. Truant.

You can email him at <u>david@sterlingandstone.net</u>
We swear, he almost never bites. Unless you feed him
after midnight.

Also By Nolon King

Hidden Justice

Hidden Justice

Hidden Honor

Hidden Shame

Hidden Virtue

No Justice

No Justice

No Escape

No Hope

No Return

No Stopping

No Fear

Once Upon A Crime

Once Upon A Crime

Twice Upon A Lie

Three Times a Murder

Dead For Good

Dead For Good

Left For Dead

Dead Of Night

Wake The Dead

Dead For Life

Stand Alone Novels

Pretty Killer

12

Blown

Miserable Lies

The Target

Secrets We Keep

Close To Home

Heat To Obsession

A Simple Kill

Tell Me No Lies

Red Carpet Black

Fade To Black

Victim

Also By David W. Wright

Hidden Justice

Hidden Justice

Hidden Honor

Hidden Shame

Hidden Virtue

No Justice

No Justice

No Escape

No Hope

No Return

No Stopping

No Fear

Karma Police

Jumper

Karma Police

The Collectors

Deviant

The Fall

Homecoming

Yesterday's Gone

October's Gone

Yesterday's Gone Season One

Yesterday's Gone Season Two

Yesterday's Gone Season Three

Yesterday's Gone Season Four

Yesterday's Gone Season Five

Yesterday's Gone Season Six

Tomorrow's Gone

Tomorrow's Gone Season One

Tomorrow's Gone Season Two

Tomorrow's Gone Season Three

Available Darkness

Darkness Itself

Available Darkness Book One

Available Darkness Book Two

Available Darkness Book Three

WhiteSpace

WhiteSpace Season One

WhiteSpace Season Two

WhiteSpace Season Three

Stand Alone Novels

12

Crash

Emily's List

Threshold